T0208829

Chronicles of Azelia

E.A. CALHOUN

authorHOUSE®

AuthorHouse™
1663 Liberty Drive
Bloomington, IN 47403
www.authorhouse.com
Phone: 1 (800) 839-8640

Published by AuthorHouse 02/26/2019

ISBN: 978-1-7283-0118-1 (sc)
ISBN: 978-1-7283-0116-7 (hc)
ISBN: 978-1-7283-0117-4 (e)

Library of Congress Control Number: 2019902005

Prologue

On a fiery planet known as Azelia, a town at the foot of a volcano is bustling with humanoids running their daily errands. Large dragons soar through the sky, most circling above a large crimson castle that is built into the volcano itself. The castle has ducts carrying lava running through it from the volcano, providing natural heat, before pouring into a large hole at the base of the castle. Above the fiery abyss rests a large balcony where ceremonies are held. Inside the castle sits a woman with long, wavy blue hair and blue eyes, named Akira, who is wearing a silky blue night gown as she reads her young daughter, Aurica, a bedtime story. Aurica, who has a pixie face surrounded by reddish-brown hair and crimson eyes, is also wearing a night gown, but hers is a deep red to match her eyes. The room is a pale red and holds her bed, a dresser with a vanity mirror, a closet, and an entire corner littered with soft fluffy animal toys her father gave her. In another corner there are scorch marks on the stone from practicing her magic. There is a crimson chandelier hanging from the ceiling with flames that will burn day and night, unless the flow of lava is stopped. Most of the rooms in this large cavern-like castle are similar in appearance, the differences depending upon who occupies the room.

"A long time ago, before dragon humanoids, mighty dragons, with their respective powers, lived on a planet called Simiera. These dragons flew freely and effortlessly through the universe. There were twelve elemental dragons, plus four others that we have never known much about. Though occasionally they would meet on Simiera, they rarely traveled together." Akira read aloud in a soft and gentle voice.

Aurica tugged lightly on her mother's sleeve and asked in a curious tone, "Is Azelia the same as Simiera?"

Akira smiled as she shook her head, quietly explaining, "No Aurica, it's not, but I'll get to that… Their solar system is smaller than ours, with a blue super giant star at its center, surrounded by Simiera and two other rocky planets, as well as two gas planets."

Aurica began rubbing her eyes as she grew tired, but forced herself to stay awake. Akira waited patiently until her daughter had settled and was once again focused, before she continued the story. "During their travels, they would encounter many other lifeforms in the other solar systems that made up their spiral galaxy; one that had many names from the different inhabitants within it. One name; given by a species who called themselves human, was the Milky Way galaxy. The dragons had been to Ariliria many times, but each time the humans didn't react well to their presence." The excitement built, reflected in her voice, as she loved telling this part. "*So ironic.*" Akira thought to herself, as she thought of her husband.

"That's where dad is from!!" Aurica exclaimed as she slid from her bed and ran towards the decorated door. Shaking her head as her daughter continued into the hallway, Akira put the book down and went after her, softly calling her name. She lost sight of Aurica, but found her youngest, a slight boy with cool blue hair and similar eyes, wandering around.

"Raiko? What are you doing up?" Akira asked in a calm voice.

The boy rubbed his eyes as he peered up at his mother and mumbled, "I couldn't sleep mom, and Aurica is up."

Taking his hand and leading him back the way he'd come, Akira realized that her hyperactive daughter had run down that way as well when the girl's giggle reached her ears. Noticing that Raiko had begun to fall back asleep while walking, she wished that her daughter would follow suit, thinking, "*Of all the nights for her to not go to sleep easily.*"

Akira walked down the castles' corridor that led to her and her husband's room, noticing that the door was open and she could easily hear Aurica and Jeticous' voices.

"…And that was the story! Did you know??" Aurica exclaimed excitedly. Jeticous, her father, simply nodded his head, and looked up to see Akira and Raiko coming towards them. Yawning as he pulled away to run towards his father, Raiko tripped and began to fall, giving a small cry as the floor rushed up at him. Akira moved quickly, catching him by pure reflex as she gently and effortlessly picked him up. Aurica ran up to her mother and brother with a huge smile on her face until she noticed the older woman's disapproving look. She apologized, and with her head down, returned to her room.

Jeticous raised his hand to his head, and with an exhausted breath softly said, "I wonder when that'll wear off..."

"Your guess it as good as mine at this point," Akira replied with a gentle shrug, so as not to wake Raiko who had passed out.

Jeticous walked over to her, kissed her cheek and looked down at his son, murmuring, "Akira, you should go to sleep, I'll take Raiko. It is a big day tomorrow, after all."

Nodding as her husband took the boy from her, she turned and headed toward their bed but paused to turn back around before Jeticous left, calling, "Jet, talk to her?"

He nodded with an uneasy smile and left the room with a sigh. After bringing Raiko to his room and tucking the boy back into bed, he went to Aurica's room, to find that she was hiding under the blankets, awake and alert. Jet sighed and announced. "There seems to be a mole in my daughter's bed! I shall squish it!!"

Aurica began to giggle and shuffled around under the sheet, laughing wildly. Jet dropped onto the bed and tried to catch her, eventually getting ahold of her and exclaiming, "I have caught the little rodent! My daughter can now sleep in peace, for she has a very big day in the morning!"

The giggles finally subsided as she realized that the serious talk was about to start. He uncovered her head and pulled her onto his lap. "Aurica, you know what tomorrow is, right? I know you get excited, but you *are* a princess, and tomorrow marks a new day in all of your lives." She simply nodded. He continued softly by questioning, "Will you go to sleep now?" Waiting until she simply nodded, he hugged her and turned to leave, telling her, "I love you."

~~~~~~

That night Queen Akira was in her study, writing in her diary as she had for most of her life. "*Time has sped by. Raiko is about to celebrate his eighth birthday, Aurica is eleven and Phykira is twenty-one.*" She stopped and thought to herself before adding. "*I can't believe that my eldest daughter is twenty-one. When I was her age, I was already married and pregnant with her. I suppose I had no choice, as I was an only child, but I know it frustrates her that*

Jet and I have forced her to wait. I can tell that she's fallen in love with her guard, Vincent. He's a fine young man, but something feels off… He's been leaving the castle frequently. I know that it's making Phykira nervous as well, but probably not in the same way."

"On the other hand, Zander has been Aurica's guard for a few years now, and even though he is still relatively new at it, he's doing very well. They seem to be fond of each other, but I know it's more of a brother-sister bond. Prince Conrad has grown so much recently. He loves Aurica; there is no doubt in my mind that he would never allow harm to befall her, and he's not as mean as he used to be. Aurica has changed him for the better without either of them realizing it. Raiko has never been as rambunctious as Aurica was; he's timid and likes to pretend he's a ninja.

"The dragons are all doing great, and all three of them usually get along. However, being opposites, Calcifer and Glacey do have some disagreements about certain points. It's almost time for the three children to come face to face with Ignis, and he hasn't revealed his choice to me. My feelings about this matter are clear; no matter which one of them is chosen, I know the other two will help. I honestly think it'll be Aurica; she's mischievous, but she cares about this world and the others in our system; and Ignis mentions her frequently…"

Part 1

The Destruction

On a fiery and intense planet called Azelia; home of the Fire dragons and the royal family that governed the entire solar system, a ceremony was taking place. It was the coronation of the new ruler, who would be chosen from the royal family's three children. In the Azelian society, the Queen or King was chosen based on the compatibility of the individual with Ignis, the Fire Dragon who resides underneath the capital castle of Azelia. The volcano itself was enormous; with a brilliant crimson castle that glistened in the sunlight built into the East side, and had lava ducts coursing through it.

Millions of dragon-humanoids began to gather below the balcony in anticipation, and hundreds of dragons hovered effortlessly in the air. The whole area was bustling with excitement; the dragons waiting patiently as the humanoids laughed and joked as they crowded together outside of the castle. They could see their Queen; a beautiful woman with long, wavy light-blue hair and blue eyes, wearing the ceremonial dress of her station. The dress is blue, like her hair, with the symbols and colors of the other dragon elements embroidered on the belt around her ribs. She waits patiently as everyone settles, motioning for her husband to join her, which he reluctantly does. Unlike his wife and everyone else in this solar system, he is a human from Ariliria.

In the castle, a young girl with reddish brown hair and crimson eyes is sneaking around the castle dressed in a red tunic. She is the younger princess, the second of the royal heirs, and the most mischievous. She sneaks past some of the guards, as she isn't ready for the ceremony and couldn't care less about it; all she wants is to go flying around with her dragon, Calcifer, before the ceremony and make a flashy entrance. Her wings are crimson; like her eyes, and almost completely transparent as well as detached from her.

Sneaking around a corner, she crept onto a side balcony; which it was small and not very popular due to its size. She hadn't done a very good job at sneaking, because before she could jump off the balcony, a guard named Vincent caught her and pulled her down. Her older sister was there, with her arms crossed over her chest as she glared down at the younger girl. The other girl had black hair that was the same length as their mothers, dark eyes with a hint of blue and she was wearing a beautiful black dress. Vincent wore a gray guards' uniform, with his honors decorating his chest. He had long, gray hair that was pulled into a loose braid that accentuated his yellow-green eyes.

Aurica silently went to Phykira and took her punishment, which was a simple tap on the head. Any further discussion was interrupted by the sound of whooshing air that came from the balcony behind them. Turning, they found the princesses' dragons; Abyss and Calcifer, hovering in mid-air. Abyss was quite large, but not yet full-grown; with scales that were like shimmering midnight and eyes so dark he appeared to have no pupils. Calcifer was officially an adult, but he was small compared to Abyss. He was a beautiful red, with blue flames stretching over his back, neck, head and wings. Aside from the blue flames, he looked like a normal fire dragon. Aurica was excited to see him, as they had been kept apart as punishment after they had decided to fly further than they were supposed to the day before.

Vincent smirked and strutted to the balcony, sneering at the dragons as he ordered them to go to the main balcony for the ceremony. Both continued to hover in the air for several seconds, glaring at Vincent, before looking to the princesses to whom they were bound; and receiving subtle nods, whirled away to await the beginning of the ceremony.

After the dragons left, Vincent led them way from the temptation of the balcony, and found Zander waiting for them down the hall. Zander was thirteen now and quite tall, and he had black hair with silver at the tips that was cut in a short and spiky style. He wore a guard's formal uniform, which was less protective, but looked nicer. He pushed himself away from the wall and moved into step next to Aurica when they drew even with him. They continued through the corridors, and as they approached the long hall to the main balcony they saw Akira, Jet and Raiko waiting for them; all three of them in proper ceremonial attire.

Aurica, realizing that she was not dressed properly, snapped her wings out and turned back towards the family's living quarters, jumped into the air and began flying hurriedly through the castle to her room. She found the panicked maids waiting for her outside of her room, who, upon seeing her, immediately grabbed her arm to pull her into the bedchamber. The experienced maids had her ready in minutes, and knowing that they didn't have the time to style Aurica's hair the way they had planned, settled for a simple braid instead. Her dress is was simple; red, with blue ruffles underneath, and the head maid quickly threaded ribbons to match the dress through the princess' hair. Studying her reflection in the mirror, Aurica nodded happily, quickly offered her thanks and rushed to the balcony.

~~~~~~

The heir was finally going to be decided from Queen Akira's three children. Her oldest, Phykira, was twenty-one and was a darkness dragon with beautiful jet black hair and eyes, and skin that was pale and clear. She wore an undecorated black dress that went just past her knees, with her onyx jewel as a head piece. The second child was Aurica, a fire dragon, who was eleven, and wore her ruby jewel that matched her dress as a necklace. The third child was a boy named Raiko. He had just turned eight, the age one had to be to for the ceremony to happen regardless of the older children's ages. He was an ice dragon with gray-blue hair and pale blue eyes. He wore black pants, a gray shirt, with a blue cloak that was draped over him, and he always covered his mouth with a mask. Phykira took the mask off as he arrived, and he didn't do anything to get it back, knowing that his father would have taken it if his sister hadn't.

Akira finished her speech and stood waiting for her children to come onto the balcony. Akira was a water dragon and the current Queen of the Azcerek solar system. She had wavy blue hair and pale blue eyes. Her second husband; and the father of Aurica and Raiko, stood next to her smiling back at his children. He was proud of all three of them, and hoped that regardless of who was chosen, the others would support the new leader. Jet had dark brown hair and green eyes, and wore the royal garb of the king.

Aurica was panting slightly as she scurried to the side of her sister and brother. Akira had extended her speech to give her more time, as she had figured that her most hyperactive child was going to be late. Again. After she had composed herself, she gave a nearly imperceptible nod and the three of them walked past their parents to the edge of the balcony and waved to the thousands of humanoid dragons and the dragons in the sky celebrating.

The ground started rumbling; but no one seemed to panic, in fact, their cheering became louder as Ignis; the fire dragon who partnered with the founder of Azelia, came out of the cave below the balcony. He turned toward the candidates and lowered his head to meet their eyes. Everyone became silent as the three heirs bowed, backed away and stood straight waiting for the next instructions. Ignis breathed onto the balcony and a pillar of light shot up, illuminating the stone. After a moment he telepathically said. *"Phykira, you shall go first."*

She stepped into the light, and when nothing happened, she elegantly bowed and began walked back towards her shocked younger siblings. Ignis then ordered Raiko to come next, but yet again nothing happened. Raiko rejoined his sisters, however he was smiling at the fact that if it wasn't him or Phykira, then it had to be his sister Aurica.

Sure enough after she walked into the pillar, it lit up brighter and turned maroon, causing everyone gathered to begin cheering. Aurica couldn't believe it; she didn't *want* to be the ruler. She tried to look back at Phykira, but Ignis drew her attention back to him as he requested, *"Aurica, hold out your pendant."*

She did as he asked; holding it out toward him so that his flames fused with it and it took the shape of a crescent moon.

"Aurica you may now…" Ignis began, only to be interrupted by the sound of a ship soaring above them. The screams of the frightened citizens mingled with the shouts of the royal guard as those gathered ran in all directions. Within minutes the unidentified ship had netted hundreds of dragons; forcing the large beasts to the ground, and began charging for a blast. Encumbered by the crowd and his enormous body, Ignis didn't have time to react before the ship fired upon them. The blast destroyed most of the right side of the castle, and in the confusion, a male figure descended a rescue line, quickly nabbing Aurica before heading back to the ship while everyone else was still panicking.

Phykira gave chase immediately, trying to determine who had dared to disrupt a ceremony so vital to the continued existence of Azelia and its inhabitants. He was masked; making it impossible to tell who he was or what type of dragon he happened to be, with any hair he may have tucked away behind a hood. Hearing someone behind him, he briefly turned around to face Phykira and her dragon Abyss, as Aurica's dragon Calcifer arrived to help, and realizing that he was outmatched, continued his retreat to the waiting ship.

Spotting the coward that had taken Aurica, Calcifer's eyes became a deeper red and full of rage; the fire jets on his body going into overdrive as he caught up to them. Abyss released his powers to the left of the man and toward the ship in an effort to stop him, while Calcifer charged after Abyss' attack in the hopes the man would loosen the tight grip he had on Aurica.

The ship suddenly released a beam to help the man, who seemed to be doing something he was using Aurica's body to hide. Narrowing her eyes at the abductors actions, Phykira decided to find out. She charged at him, but he dodged away from her, only to be kicked in the back by Raiko. Unfortunately, Raiko's kick didn't have the desired effect, allowing the abductor to blast both of them while he cautiously moved back toward the ship. Seeing that Ignis was preparing an attack, he decided to stop playing around and took off for the ship once more.

He almost made it to the ship with Aurica, but risking herself; Phykira came in from his upper left, swooped down and pushed Aurica out of his arms. He tried to turn to retrieve her, but Phykira grabbed his arm, jerking him backwards. He grunted as he hit the ground, and seeing who his assailant was, jumped to his feet before swiftly knocking her out, lifting her into his arms and running with her into the ship.

Calcifer had caught Aurica as she fell and had taken to the air to remove her from the battle. He was heading back down towards the remains of the castle, when the ship started firing at him, forcing him to fly away from safety as he began to feel the effect of his overdrive and the desperate need to land. They continued high into the atmosphere, making it impossible for Raiko and Zander; who were searching for Phykira, to reach them.

Inside of the ship there were two men; the one who had tried to abduct Aurica but settled for Phykira, and the one controlling the ship and firing at Calcifer. The pilot was making no attempt to mask himself, and his short, spiky silver hair and gray-yellow eyes stood out. He seemed to be enjoying himself, while the other waited for an opportunity to recapture Aurica. They continued forcing Calcifer out of Azelia's atmosphere, thus forcing Raiko to back off as he wasn't yet strong enough for high-altitude flying and was quickly becoming exhausted. He knew that if he continued his ascent, he might be more of a burden when those searching for his sisters were forced to rescue him.

Zander was on an ice dragon that Aurica had befriended as a child and was able to go much further than Raiko could. He continued to look around for Phykira, and watched to see if he could help with Aurica. Akira and many of the other dragons had taken to the sky and were beginning to make their way to them, offering him hope that both girls would be recovered.

Meanwhile, the masked abductor held onto the ship, shouting at his companion. "Stop playing Klaus!"

Klaus sighed dramatically and began a full assault on Calcifer; who had been hit a few too many times and was running out of energy. He was making every effort to keep them in Azelia's atmosphere, but Klaus wasn't going easy on him anymore.

Ignis had joined the battle, and firing a blast, blew a huge chunk of the ship away. Unfortunately the resulting explosion and debris blew Calcifer and Aurica away; completely out of the atmosphere, at a high rate of speed. At the sight of the huge dragon, the men in the ship decided to retreat with Phykira still on board.

Watching as the ship escaped into space, Ignis lowered his head in defeat, as did many in the crowd. Akira had arrived in time to protect her son and Zander, but both her daughters were gone. With tears in her eyes she stared out into deep space, her unconscious son cradled in her arms. Zander landed with the others and slid from the back of the ice dragon that had assisted him, softly offering his thanks.

Abyss was gone as well, having chased after the ship on his own in an effort to rescue Phykira. Akira reached the surface and handed Raiko to Jeticous, before walking to the balcony to get her people's attention. Forcing authority into her voice, she requested, "Everyone, please calm down. Phykira and Aurica are both alive, and we have to assume that the assailant's intent is not to kill them. However; due to his actions, this planet is unstable. I regret that I must ask all of the representatives from the neighboring planets to leave immediately for your own safety. The citizens of Azelia are to remain here, and I will use my powers to seal all of the inhabitants of Azelia in a safe place before I prematurely detonate Azelia.

Hopefully the blast will help Aurica to land safely on another planet. King Elefon, I ask that you put a barrier of protection around the other planets in our system."

"If only the planet had stabilized sooner... But sadly, the scars of the war are ever present." Akira murmured.

~~~~~~

Everyone did as she requested; the dragons from the other planets quickly left and the inhabitants of Azelia waited patiently. When only the Azelians remained, Akira began securing the citizens in a device she and Ignis had designed long ago, as the great dragon used the last of his powers to aid her. While his wife was seeing to the safety of their people, Jeticous ordered Raiko's dragon, Glacey, to chase after Aurica and Calcifer. The boy, having awakened during his mother's speech, left with the dragons, accompanied by a young girl with black hair and yellow-orange eyes. Raiko urged the others to hurry, as he was anxious to search for his sisters.

After the children had exited Azelia's atmosphere, Jet walked to his wife's side and smiled. A flash of light passed over them, leaving Akira, Jeticous and Ignis alone on the balcony. Jeticous lifted Akira into his arms, holding her securely as Ignis began to fly in fast circles around them, purposely smacking the ground with his enormous tail before pounding it will all of his weight. The planet began to tremble; the vibrations growing with each impact of Ignis' body, until the planet exploded, sending an enormous shockwave through the solar system.

Elefon used his powers to shield all of the planets in the wave's path, as well as Raiko and the other travelers. Their dragons used the shockwave in hopes of catching up to Aurica. At one point Glacey thought she saw what looked like Calcifer in the distance, but it turned out to be a red giant instead. With no other leads they decided to head that way, using Raiko's genetic link to his sister to try to sense Aurica and Calcifer.

~~~~~~

Temporarily stunned both physically and mentally from the planets destruction, the masked man growled, "Damn she got away! Klaus turn the ship around; we have to go after her immediately!"

Klaus nodded, leaving his companion alone with Phykira, who was still unconscious. Staring down at his unexpected prisoner, the abductor muttered, "She's not going to take this well. I guess I'll wait until she wakes up and go from there. I might have to use my power on her... not that I would mind having her do what *I* said for once."

He picked her up and brought her to his room; carrying her gently and carefully through the narrow corridors, to where the door was already open. His room was a normal size; undecorated, as their ships were considered disposable. He gently placed her on his bed and backed away, muttering, "You can sleep in here for now, but I'll have to find another place to put you."

Having the ability to seal any of the rooms on the ship; he sealed the door behind him and returned to the cockpit.

Shortly after, Phykira woke up startled, glancing wildly around as her mind raced with a million questions. *"Where am I? What happened?"* She slowly got off the bed and went to the door, jerking her hand back as it shocked her. Narrowing her eyes as she backed away from the door, she recalled, *"That's right, the ones that tried to abduct Aurica captured me instead... Oh, Aurica, I hope you're ok, but right now I have to figure out how to get out of here before who ever put me in here comes back... the question is; how?"*

Pulled from her musings as she heard a voice say "unlock.", she gasped, *"He's here!"*

The door opened and Phykira charged towards her kidnapper, stopping when she saw Vincent; a guard from Azelia's castle, and the man she had trusted and begun to love. Anger flooding her, she flew into motion, almost hitting him, but he grabbed her arm and twisted her body so that her back was to his front.

"It was you?! Why did you do this Vincent?" she demanded, her voice cracking and full of pure anguish as she was barely able to muster the words. He released her arm and she turned to face him; her face filled with anger and confusion.

Without flinching and with a straight face he replied, "That's easy. I'm a time dragon and I wanted your sweet little sister to reform Cerek, the world of the time dragons. I've had to wait until she was old enough, and chosen to be the new ruler of Azelia, of course. I was hoping that it would be you, which would have been much easier for both of us, but I was doomed to disappointment."

At his words she turned away from him, whispering, "So all of this time you were just using me?"

He Vincent grabbed her shoulder and leaned into her body. "At first that was all I cared about, but you've become someone I care about too. I have to tell you something, and you aren't going to like it."

She immediately thought of Aurica. "What happened to Aurica? Is she ok?"

Vincent let go and walked ahead of her. "Relax, I think the little brat is fine, however; Azelia blew up. That was not part of my plan. I was planning on threatening Azelia if Aurica didn't comply."

"Azelia is gone?" Wide eyed, she fell back to the bed, her hands covering her face as she struggled to accept his words. Turning over what he'd said in her mind, she suddenly stood back up, her fierce eyes directly meeting his as she demanded, "Wait! Did Aurica make it back to the planet?! Where is she?!"

As Vincent shook his head, Phykira bit back a sob and forced herself to calm down as she looked down at the floor. "*Then I'm a bargaining chip...*"

Raising her gaze to meet his, asked sternly, "So that's why you took me?"

He laughed as he reached to cup her face. "I would have taken you regardless, Princess; I had gotten rid of all the obstacles after all."

She hit his hand away and he shrugged with a smirk. Angry with herself for falling for his act, she turned away and saw the door wide open. Glancing from him to the door, she thought, "*There is no way I could outrun him, but it's worth a try.*"

Vincent didn't move, just continued to smirk at her. Gritting her teeth, she demanded, "Are you responsible for what happened to Aurica too?"

His smirk faded as he nodded. Phykira grew even more furious, and looking back at the open door, clearly telegraphed her intentions. Following her eyes to the open door, he held his hand out just past Phykira's head, yelling, "Shut! Seal!"

Turning his gaze to the young woman now glaring at him, he taunted, "You aren't thinking of running now are you? Remember all that time we've spent together? I studied you, and now I know all of your moves and actions, sweetheart. If you try to escape, I can finally show you how I truly am."

~~~~~~~

The morning after Azelia's destruction Phykira woke up with Vincent's arm around her waist. Nothing had happened between them; he had shown his true colors, but he still wasn't that much of a low life. Phykira had cried most of the night, and though Vincent sat on the bed and took her punches, he didn't say much more than he had already divulged. Whenever Azelia's destruction came up he apologized, but he wouldn't apologize for trying to kidnap Aurica or for what happened to her. Phykira didn't move as she continued to think about what happened, and what Vincent had said last night. Closing her eyes against the truth of her situation, she silently questioned, *"Aurica, are you alive? You can reform Azelia; I know you can, but you're going to need help finding the dragons. Hold on and I'll do whatever it takes to find you... Without leading Vincent to you, I hope..."*

Vincent woke up and noticed Phykira was awake as well, but lost in thought; so much so, that she hadn't realized he'd awakened. Turning to her, he softly inquired, "Phykira? Do you have any more questions?"

She shook her head, so he shrugged and got up. He found his shirt; a white tunic that was half-undone, and pulled it over his head. She had risen as well, and he walked over to her, staring at her until she met his eyes. "I can tell I'm going to have to use my powers on you. I was hoping that you would not be a pain, but apparently you're going to be just like Aurica. Who, by the way, you're going to help me find, my love."

She blushed at the endearment, and the half-undone shirt wasn't helping her any either. "What do you mean? I won't help you; you're going to hurt her."

Vincent was smiling. "Do you know the powers of the time dragons?"

She shook her head again. She had heard mixed things; most elemental dragons had 1-2 different powers beside their obvious one, but the time dragons were mysterious, and if the rumors were true, they had the ability to brainwash people by kissing them. If they kissed their victim on the lips, it was everlasting unless the person had a strong will. *"No way could that be one, that's just too strange; plus, I have a strong will."*

She was blushing even more at the thought of him kissing her. He was smirking at first, but she was turning so red he began to get concerned. "Ahh, Phykira? What in the world are you thinking about?"

Vincent leaned in close to her and she fell over in a panic. "W-what are you doing? No I don't know; I've only heard rumors!"

He extended his hand to help her up. "What have you heard? It might be true; I've never brought up the time dragons in the castle, so I truly don't know what they say about us."

She had taken his hand but then backed away and turned around. She stared at the blank wall, and in a soft voice, answered, "The ability to wrap time of course, putting up special barriers that can also stop time in a given area, and if one kisses someone on the lips they'll be under that time dragon's control."

He closed his eyes and smirked. "Well, what do you know...? All of that is true."

Phykira tensed as Vincent put his hand on her shoulder and turned her around, inquiring, "Want to give it a try? You can personally see for yourself that it's true... Not that you have much of a choice; I just don't want your first time being kissed to be forced."

She didn't either. *There is no way out of it so I might as well enjoy it*.

She looked up at him and closed her eyes. He half-hugged her as she wrapped her arms around him and he bent down to touch his lips to hers. With a sigh, Phykira melted into his embrace.

Several minutes later he let her go and stepped away. "Phykira? It worked, sweetheart, but don't worry, as it won't last long. Once you have given up on escaping and helping Aurica; it'll fade. I guess I'll have to wait until then, as it's no fun being in a relationship with someone who's under your control."

Klaus walked in laughing. "I have to disagree with you on that, brother, but then again I don't have to use that ability too often either. You should ask Phykira if she can sense Aurica; see if we can find her so we can be done with this... Or at least go somewhere, anywhere, I can flirt with girls."

Slightly annoyed, Vincent faced Phykira again. "Phykira where is Aurica? Can you sense her?"

Klaus walked over to them as Phykira nodded. Exchanging glances, they looked at each other and then back at her, demanding in unison, "Where?"

"In the direction of Ariliria, but she hasn't landed on any planet yet."

Klaus left to go see if any of their associates were out that way.

Taking the princess' hand, Vincent led her into the corridor, stating, "Come on Phykira, you don't need to be locked up anymore, let's go find Aurica."

She nodded and followed him to the control room. Pausing behind the other man as he studied the display in front of the pilot, Vincent growled, "Who is out that way right now? Aren't those ten brothers near there?"

Klaus nodded and pointed to a series of planets. "I already told them to search in this sector and alert me if they find anything, but... Let's join them over there; see if we can find a little bit of fun."

Feeling Phykira stiffen at his side, Vincent nodded with a smile. "Yes, let's see what treasures Ariliria holds for us..."

~~~~~~

Almost a month had gone by since Aurica's attempted abduction and the explosion of Azelia. When Calcifer had regained consciousness after drifting through outer space, he realized that there was a barrier around them, but it wasn't going to last much longer. He recognized their general position and flew toward the relative safety of Ariliria. As Aurica remained unconscious and didn't awaken for the whole trip, Calcifer rarely stopped to rest. With his battle-weakened speed and inability to refuel properly, it took close to a year to reach Arilirias' solar system, and while she still showed no signs of waking up, Calcifer knew that she was still alive. He had also noticed distant figures following them on several occasions, but had managed to evade them as he traveled as fast as he was able. Due to the shock of the abduction, explosion, and then being hurdled into empty space, she had unconsciously put herself into a coma-like stasis. Luckily Calcifer found small planets with water along the way and was able to keep Aurica hydrated.

Glacey and Raiko; who had also become unconscious, had gravitated toward Ariliria as well. She saw Calcifer in the distance and attempted to catch up with him, but he had already entered Ariliria's atmosphere and begun to descend rapidly. At an observatory on Ariliria, two objects were sighted hurtling toward the planet's surface; one red, and the other blue with sliver spirally around it. The observers braced for impact, hiding under the cluttered desk, completely astonished that what had appeared to be comets, had come out of nowhere and with such velocity. Dust had enveloped everything within a five-mile radius of the initial impact area. The other landed lightly nearby.

Calcifer; weak from the journey, had crashed into a forest clearing near a small town. It was summer, with the sun's powerful rays beating down on them, and lifting his head toward the light, he absorbed the heat just as he had the whole time they had been out in space, taking energy from the numerous stars they had passed on their journey. He had finally run out of energy on their descent and had hit the ground with uncontrolled force, barely managing to extend his wing over Aurica before passing out.

When Aurica awoke with a gasp, all she could see was a dim, reddish light all around her. She didn't know where she was, but it felt weird and she was having trouble breathing, although not enough for true concern. The red walls surrounding her started to shift and she suddenly realized that Calcifer was covering her with one of his giant wings. His wings were essentially fire jets; often used as a means of defense in battle, and after years of practice he could control the heat and the direction of the output.

Receiving no reaction to her movements, she instinctively reached out for his mind, instantly relieved to find he was just exhausted and not seriously injured. Calcifer was happy to find that Aurica was finally awake, and shifting his body, lifted his wing so she could crawl out. She rose cautiously, almost falling over from the muscle weakness and malnourishment caused by the stasis she'd been in during their journey. She managed to get her footing and looked around again, immediately knowing that she was no longer on Azelia, but a planet that she did recognize. Arıliria. Her father's planet, and the place where he had met Phykira's father; King Kuron, many years before. Kuron had sympathized with the humans, and left Azelia to help them in their war against the strange monsters that had begun to invade their world.

Aurica spotted two figures coming out of the brush, and as the temperature dropped, she recognized her brother's presence and ran over to them. Glacey had had chosen to don her human form and was easily carrying the unconscious boy in her arms. She had pale blue hair and eyes, and wore a royal blue overcoat, with mittens and a white hat that rested upon her head. Checking her younger brother over carefully, Aurica demanded, "Is he alright? Why isn't he waking up?"

Biting back a sharp retort aimed at her new queen, Glacey replied, "Raiko is fine. He was forced to place himself in stasis for our journey. He said that he would awaken within minutes of an atmospheric change, which should be any time now."

Nodding at the dragon's words, Aurica said, "That makes sense… I'm sorry for my harsh tone, Glacey; I was just concerned for Raiko. I meant no offense."

"None taken, your majesty." Placing Raiko carefully on the ground, Glacey offered Aurica a slight bow of respect before turning to Calcifer to add, "I'm pleased to see that you survived the battle and journey."

Calcifer, who had also switched to his human form, nodded weakly, adding, "Though not unscathed."

Glacey began to speak, only to whirl around and face the direction from which she and Raiko had come from, her eyes scanning the forest repeatedly before locking onto two forms weaving through the trees. Raiko was still passed out where Glacey had set him down; and she moved to sit next to him, ready to protect him from any threat. Calcifer rose as quickly as he was able and went to stand with Aurica, who had also noticed the strangers. Though weary, they prepared themselves for a potential battle, silently hoping that they had enough energy between the three of them to survive.

A couple suddenly stumbled through the brush, patting themselves and looking curiously around. Spotting the small group, they offered bright smiles before growing concerned by their appearance. Due to the year spent drifting through space, they had grown considerably, and their clothes were not only too small, but tattered and torn, with smudges of dirt and dust from the impact as well.

The couple slowly walked over to the now loosely gathered children, the woman cautiously removing medical kit from her pack and raising a questioning eyebrow as a silently request to treat them. When Aurica nodded and pointed to her dragon, the woman began treating Calcifer, wincing at the level of exhaustion that filled the young man.

Darting glances at the man as his companion evaluated her dragon; Aurica noted that the man had dark brown hair and green eyes, just like her father. In fact, he looked so much like Jet, that when she first saw him she thought that he had somehow followed them. The woman who was treating Calcifer had red hair and green eyes and was wearing a skirt and a t-shirt. After several minutes Calcifer told her that he was fine, but she wouldn't hear it; and watching as she pulled items from her bag, Aurica and Calcifer were surprised by how prepared she was.

The man who looked like her father spoke calmly to her. "Are you alright? Please don't worry about your friend. My wife, Kim, is a doctor and one of the best."

Aurica had been staring at him curiously, nodding as he spoke, but now she was concentrating on Calcifer, trying to stay focused. She was attempting to heal him telepathically, which was working until Calcifer noticed, glaring at her until she looked away. The man looked at them curiously, but let it go as he bent down to offer, "Oh by the way I'm Raven. May I ask your name?"

She had been studying him again, and at his words, nodded and rose to her feet as he did the same. She cleared her throat and answered, "My name is Aurica." Pointing to her companions, she added, "That's Calcifer, the blue haired girl is Glacey and the boy is my brother, Raiko."

Raven smiled and nodded, but didn't say anything, seeming to be lost in thought. The sun had begun to descend after Kim had treated Aurica, Raiko and Glacey. Raiko still hadn't awakened and while Calcifer and Glacey each wanted to carry him if the other couldn't, they were both too exhausted and Aurica wasn't yet strong enough either. Raven solved the building argument by lifting the boy into his arms and carrying him back towards their home as Kim told them the history of the town.

"Our town is called Jade town, and it's a nice place to live, with a reservoir lake called Lake Greenwood. After the last war; when the planet's remaining citizens voted to rename it Ariliria, the residents of our village also voted to rename our town. Sort of a new beginning all the way around, you know? Right now, you're in Emerald province, which is located on the southeastern corner of a continent we now call Lorelle."

Aurica was listening carefully, again thinking how prepared they were and how unsurprised they were to see them. *"She's explaining this to me so carefully, as if she knows I'm not from this planet. Who are these people, and why does Raven look like my father??"*

They arrived in the evening, when the streets were fairly lit and the town still bustling; it was cluttered and organized at the same time. The houses on the outskirts were mainly farming families who supplied food for the town, growing indigo and rice with a few other crops thrown in. As they moved closer into town there were fewer individual family houses, and more apartment complexes and tall buildings. They didn't go to the taller buildings, as Raven and Kim lived in the apartments.

Their apartment was clean, organized and ready to receive visitors. They had a spare bedroom, where they placed Raiko, with Glacey staying in the room with him as Kim continued to treat him. Raven was once again talking to Aurica and he seemed a bit hesitant in asking his questions. When he had finished getting the room situated to his satisfaction, he returned to the living room, where Aurica and Calcifer were waiting. He sat down, took a deep breath and met her confused gaze before he asked, "Would your father happen to be Jeticous?"

Fire dragons

Red to blue scales in color, though being born a blue dragon
spells a short life, much like a blue giant star. They are rash in
nature; usually acting before thinking. They embrace power above
all else, often throwing their immense power around.

They don't bond with humanoids very often, as they see them as weaknesses.

The fire humanoids, reddish brown or red hair, warm colored eyes ranging
from red to yellow, tanned skin to dark skin. Some cases of lighter skin.

Planet name: Azelia

Ruler Aurica

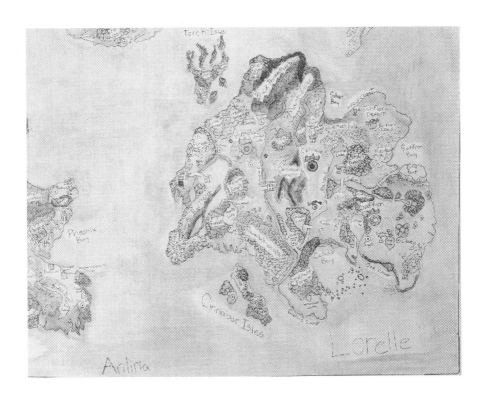

Part 2

A New Life

Aurica nodded and looked at him with wide eyes. While her father was from Ariliria, he hadn't been back many times, and she had only been with him a few times. He smiled, looked as though he was about to speak but hesitated, and rising, he moved to the guest room to see how Kim was doing. She frowned, pushing him out into the hall and whispering for him to just tell her. He reluctantly walked back to Aurica and sat down again.

She stared at him until he spoke again, and knowing she wasn't going to let it go, he said, "He's...my father too."

Aurica didn't say anything, just sat there completely stunned. He continued thinking; struggling, to find the answers to the questions he knew that she was thinking. "He didn't know I was still alive. You see, there was a war he was involved in; the one you might have learned about."

She nodded. Phykira had told her about how her father had been involved in it and that's where Kuron and Jeticous had met and become friends. When Phykira's father was killed, his trusted comrade and friend, Jet, was allowed to come to Azelia for his funeral.

Raven continued. "My mother was seriously injured and he thought we both were dead, but I had left to find him before my mother died. But I was small and got lost, and by the time I finally made it back, it was time for her funeral." Seemingly overcome with emotion, he stopped there for the rest of the night; offering her a nod before rising and walking from the room.

Thinking of what he'd told her, she decided to accept it as truth, but only because everything was beginning to make sense.

~~~~~~

She couldn't sleep that night, worry etched on her face as she stayed up watching over Raiko; who remained unconscious. Calcifer and Glacey fought their exhaustion, but in the end, succumbed to it, leaving her to her solitary watch. She fiddled with the pendant hanging around her neck. It shone brightly and an image of her mother appeared. As she turned the stone, her father's image appeared beside Akira's, but the rest was blank. The likeness suddenly smiled and turned to meet her gaze directly as Akira said, "*Aurica, if you're seeing this, it means you've made it to another world and you're both ok. I can only pray that Raiko and Glacey have found you and are safe as well.*

"*The ship that attacked us is believed to be that of a time dragon. They are after you to take control of your power, and you cannot allow that to happen. Ignis and I have discussed our plan, and here is what you must do. First, you must find and tame all of the dragons, as you will need them. Second, I implore you to learn everything you are able to about how planets are formed, so that you won't exhaust too much of your own power by putting energy in the wrong places. This is far from an easy task, and after you start, it could take a while to actually reform the planet. But I believe in you, dear child, as does your father. Please don't worry about us. I have insured that everyone on Azelia will be safe for a few years, stored securely inside a stone sculpture that Ignis and I made many years ago. And please remember to not over-tax yourself with this quest! This is a very dangerous task and one that has to be taken slowly, or you will risk your own life. Good luck dear, and remember that your father and I love you and Raiko very much. Good bye.*"

The hologram disappeared, and Calcifer, who had awakened when the hologram began playing, closed his eyes in dismay. Aurica was both relieved and sad. Everyone on Azelia was okay, but why had her mother just said good bye; was she not safe as well? Worry for her parents and people filling her, Aurica turned to peer out the window, wondering how she was to accomplish the enormous task her mother had charged her with completing.

~~~~~~

The next morning Raven came into Raiko's room to check on him, while Kim was making breakfast for everyone. She had gone to the store very early that morning to get more food, and not knowing what dragons ate, she purchased plenty of meat just in case. For her, her husband and the children she made eggs, sausage and some toast, and provided orange or apple juice for the kids, as well as coffee for her and Raven. Aurica awakened and saw that Calcifer was sitting up, and saw that he had fallen asleep as he sat against the bed. She slipped from the bed without waking him, and went to check on Raiko, finding Raven was there watching their brother, who was still sleeping. Before she could greet him, he said, "Good morning Aurica. Raiko has been mumbling and calling out your name."

He turned to her with a smile and she smiled back, thinking, '*It must be hard for him to see us; to know that Father was with us as we grew...*'

There was a long pause before he stood up; putting his hand on her shoulder and smiling again before he slipped from the room to help Kim with breakfast.

Aurica sat down on Raiko's bed; running her hand idly through his hair, when she noticed that Glacey was gone. She jumped to her feet and was about to leave when Raiko began mumbling. He sat up and rubbed his eyes, looking blurrily around the room. Aurica turned back to him; perching on the edge of his bed as she waited for him to wake enough to recognize her, before hugging him tightly. Realizing it was her, he returned the hug and jumped out of the bed without thinking; tripping over the blankets that puddled there. Aurica caught him and they shared a laugh for a brief moment, before he looked around once again, quietly saying, "So it wasn't a dream. But where are we?"

They held each other while Aurica explained what had happened, where they were, and how they were staying with Raven; who was their half-brother, and his wife Kim. They stayed huddled together until Kim announced that breakfast was ready.

No one talked much, and Raiko noticed the dragons were missing, but didn't say anything about it, as he could sense both of them nearby. After breakfast Aurica and Raiko looked around for Calcifer and Glacey; leaving the house and walking toward the forest where they both sensed their partners. Calcifer and Glacey were standing by the crash site, discussing what had happened and how the situation could be rectified. They both looked over to their companions as they approached, Calcifer studying

Aurica intensely as he asked, "What are we going to do Aurica? Should we wait for a message or…?"

She shook her head, knowing he was going to suggest going there themselves. Her mother's dragons could make the trip in a matter of days or months, depending on the distance, but Calcifer and Glacey were weaker, and too young to make the long trip again so soon. They decided to stay, recuperate and become stronger. They were in a small isolated town, and it wasn't going to get much better than that.

They returned to Raven and Kim's building, to find that they were waiting for them outside. Raiko ran to Raven and hugged his new-found brother. He looked up at Raven; his pale blue eyes meeting Raven's green eyes as he declared, "I've always wanted a brother!" The young boy then admitted that he had a good feeling about Raven because of how much he resembled Jet.

Raven was quiet for a moment before asking Raiko. "I already know this, but your name is Raiko, right?"

When the boy nodded, smiling, Raven continued by saying, "My mother was expecting a baby when she was killed, and she had always told my father and me that she wanted to name him Rai. My father loved the name, and he would always say "Raven and Rai, they are going to be fine men someday.""

Despite being sad about the tragedy of Raven's mother and younger sibling, they all had warm smiles on their faces. Raven was bending down eye to eye with Raiko, and Aurica knew that if she had to leave for any reason, that Raiko would be well taken care of and with family.

Raven and Raiko bonded quickly, and sat in the living room talking while Aurica, Calcifer and Glacey found new changes of clothes. Lunch time rolled around and the guys were still talking, so Aurica asked Kim if she needed help preparing lunch. Her sister-in-law smiled, replying, "Yes, I would love your help Aurica!"

Kim rummaged around on the counter and then handed Aurica a small bag, a list of things she needed and some money, instructing, "Go straight down the road until you see a small produce shop on the right. It's not too far but be quick if you can." Kim said hastily.

Aurica reluctantly turned to leave, but as she did, Kim stopped her and said, "Oh and Aurica, please tell them that I sent you."

Aurica nodded and left, while Calcifer stayed behind and assisted Kim in the kitchen, offering free heating and fire. Glacey watched Aurica preparing to leave; and glancing at Raiko, who was still talking to Raven, she decided to follow Aurica as Calcifer was staying at the house.

Glacey quickly caught up to Aurica, who was happy to have her along. Aurica studied her under her lashes as they walked, asking, "How am I supposed to know how much of this money I'm supposed to use for the items she wants? Dad never taught me about it."

Glacey; unable to answer the question, shrugged and they continued walking. Within minutes they could see the shopping area of the town, where many people were living an ordinary life, buying everything from groceries, to home decorations. Many of them noticed Aurica and Glacey, but minded their own business. After the events of the past, they had become very good at telling who was a threat and who wasn't. They both looked too confused and lost to be threats.

A young boy with jet black hair and eyes, and who appeared to be about Aurica's age, was walking by when he saw them, pausing to ask, "You two look lost, do you need help?"

They both nodded and told him they were on an errand for Kim. The boy led the way to the produce shop, where he went inside with them and grabbed a few things for himself. Aurica gathered the items on Kim's list and went to the counter where the boy was lingering, having already paid for his things.

Aurica had hoped to catch him before he completed his purchase so that she could see how it was done; but she figured the person who took the money would take only what she needed. She was an older woman with graying, brown hair, loose clothing and a nice welcoming smile. She put the items on the counter and the woman rang them up on a machine neither of them had ever seen before.

"That's 10.54," the woman said. Neither of them heard her, lost in their fascination of the machine. The woman managed to get their attention and repeated the amount. Embarrassed and blushing, Aurica placed the money on the counter. "I'm sorry about that, umm Kim sent me here to get this stuff."

"Oh! Is that so? That Kim! Getting children to pick up things for her now, when she usually just sends her husband. Alright... Well you gave me too much money, see? I only need this much." Aurica nodded and blushed again in embarrassment. The woman bagged the items and handed them to Aurica and Glacey. "Oh what are your names? Will you be staying long?"

Aurica smiled and replied, "I'm Aurica and she's Glacey, we'll be staying with Raven and Kim for as long as they'll let us stay, or until we figure out what to do now. What's your name?"

"My name is Carla, nice to meet you both; and such pretty names you both have!" Gesturing to where their guide lurked by the door, the cashier added, "That boy over there is named Levi."

He looked over, holding up his hand with his eyes closed and a smirk on his face.

He walked out with them, and though he didn't start any conversations, he would answer their questions. He and Aurica kept sneaking glances at each other; both thinking that they recognized the other, but neither said anything. He ran ahead of them, but suddenly turned around and stopped, advising, "You two don't look like a threat; and since you're both staying with Raven and Kim, I'm sure you're both good people, but... Be careful while you walk around the town."

He turned his face away from them; standing in a strong and stern pose, before he abruptly ran off without another word, or waiting for them to respond.

Exchanging bewildered looks, they shrugged, before heading back to Kim with the ingredients, and hoping they would get there in time, they hurried back. They found their way back easily; both could sense their partners and let that guide them back. Kim scolded them for being late, but smiled after doing it; and confused by her behavior, they offered to help prepare the ingredients. Neither of them had ever cooked before however, so Kim's kitchen turned into a giant mess. They tried to help, but continually broke things, until Kim sent them to the other room and finished preparing their meal by herself. They found Raven and Raiko still talking; they had talked through the commotion Aurica and Glacey caused, barely noticing their return. Aurica and Glacey sat beside Calcifer, who had fallen asleep while they were gone, but was awakened by the commotion.

He chuckled as they sat next to him; and after glaring at him in return, Aurica watched Raven and Raiko. They got along so well, that she was beginning to get jealous, but kept it to herself, except for Calcifer. She telepathically asked him what he thought.

'Don't take it personally Aurica. Raven didn't know that he had any siblings and when you confirmed that you were Jet's daughter, he was overwhelmed with joy.' She frowned as the mention of her father caused her to think of the fate of their parents. Unaware of the direction her thoughts had taken, Calcifer continued voicing his opinion. 'When he found out that Raiko was your brother; and therefore his too, he felt joy and sorrow. We now know the reason for that, so allow them to bond. Raven wants to get to know you just as much, but Raiko needs this bond more right now. He has you but, he needs a male figure in his life as well; and given my connection to you, he'd feel too weird talking to me about things.'

Aurica nodded and leaned on him while watching her brothers, beginning to ponder what she should do next. Calcifer, sensing the direction her thoughts had taken, chuckled, telling her softly. "Give it time, Aurica, it'll come to you."

That night, Raven cautiously asked them if they'd like to live in the village with them for a while. Aurica had thought about it; and given that a return to Azelia wasn't currently possible, it seemed like the right choice. "Yes, we'll stay with you; thank you Raven and Kim." She said happily.

Raven and Kim smiled, but they were still worried that they would leave within a couple weeks, if not days. "In that case, how would you like to go to school? You don't know much about Ariliria and how things work here, right? Our school is different from the city's schools, but you'll learn the basics of human society." Raven said excitedly. They talked for a while about how to act, what to say and so on, and hearing the requirements, Calcifer and Glacey opted out of going to school.

The next morning they reached the academy building and went into the room that Raven thought Raiko should join. The room was packed with kids Raiko's age, and they all looked over at them as they entered. After a brief conversation with the instructor, Raven and Aurica left, leaving Raiko alone. The instructor motioned Raiko forward, so he went over to her, noting that she looked nice, had dark brown hair and reminded him a lot of his mom. The instructor's name was Leslie, "I see Raven has finally found who he has been searching for! How about you tell everyone your name?"

Her words reminded him way too much of his oldest sister, but he was able to keep his cool. "Yes ma'am. My name is Raiko, and my sister and I just arrived here the other day."

Leslie looked satisfied and looked around the class room to find a seat for him. There weren't many, but after looking at some and murmuring that they wouldn't work, she spotted one by two other students; both girls, and decided he should sit there. She pointed to the seat and asked the two girls to stand up and say their names. Reluctantly they did as asked, rising slowly to their feet. The first one to speak was a brown-haired girl, whose name was Rica, followed by her companion, a slight girl with silver hair and pale blue eyes named Kairi. Raiko walked over, and as the girls welcomed him, he realized that Kairi was a bit shyer than Rica. Offering a shy smile of his own, he sat beside Kairi.

After class was done Raiko went to go find Aurica, but Leslie stopped him and said he should get to know the other students first. Hearing the instructor's words, a boy came up and asked Raiko if he wanted a tour. Raiko agreed after he saw that Leslie didn't seem to mind; he could tell she knew who would get along and who wouldn't. The boy's name was Vaan, and while he seemed to be a lot like Raiko, he was a little more outgoing. On their way out of the building they ran into Rica and Kairi. Rica waved at them and without warning, jumped high in the air and jump-kicked Vaan in the chest. He grabbed her leg and tried to toss her, but she twisted and kicked him with her other leg. They appeared to be getting out of hand and seemed to be going further than play fighting, but Kairi didn't look worried, so Raiko went to stand next to her. "I take it they do this a lot?"

Kairi nodded with an embarrassed smile and blushed a little bit. Raiko was only nine, so he didn't understand why she was turning red, and thinking she was getting too hot, suggested, "Maybe we should find a shady place."

Kairi nodded and showed him to the tree she normally sat under. Even though he was a prince, he found a decent sized leaf and fanned Kairi with it, perplexed when she started blushing even more. "Are you okay Kairi?"

She giggled a little bit. "Yeah I'm fine Raiko, thank you." Noting that Rica and Vaan had stopped fighting, Kairi realized that she had never said so many words in one sentence unless she had too.

Raiko was fascinated with her voice. '*Why doesn't she talk more often? She has such a beautiful voice, and that smile…*'

Now Raiko was the one blushing as Vaan and Rica walked over to them. "Maybe we should give you two some alone time?" Vaan suggested with a smirk. Rica punched him in the arm as Kairi blushed brightly, jumped up and ran off. Rica glared at both boys before she ran after her, and exchanging a shrug, the boys followed.

They ended up in a field with a hollowed tree trunk, to find that Kairi was hiding inside of it and Rica standing just outside of it. Raiko noticed Vaan wasn't moving any closer, so Raiko took a better look around. They could hear the girls talking and decided to wait, taking a few steps back to give them privacy. It was pretty late when Kairi came out, and with a weak smile, she apologized to all of them, relieved when they didn't mind.

"Let's head home now." Rica said, extending her hand to her friend. Kairi nodded, and taking the proffered hand, they set out together. They came across Rica's house first, and given the other girl's earlier reaction, she was reluctant to leave Kairi alone. She trusted the boys of course, but Kairi was her best friend she didn't want to have her thinking she was being lazy just because there were boys around.

Kairi, realizing the situation her friend found herself in, placed her hand on the other girl's shoulder and smile. "It's okay Rica, you just get some rest." They all looked at Kairi, and noting the other girl's smile, Rica nodded, offering a smile of her own before she turned and opened the door.

"Oh before I forget! Vaan, if you let *anything* happen to Kairi, I'll kick your butt!" Vaan blushed brightly, "You got it, Rica. I promise nothing will happen to her, ever."

She blushed, nodding as she stepped inside and closed the door. The kids continued, and the next house they came to was Vaan's; which they almost passed by, but his drunken father spotted them through the window and yelled at him to come inside. Vaan tried to explain to the older man that he made a promise to walk Kairi home safely, but his father would not hear it.

Raiko, feeling anger rise in him over the treatment his companion was receiving, quietly offered, "It is okay Vaan, I'll keep her safe and see her home."

He took Kairi's hand; which made her blush once more, as Vaan nodded with a smirk. Raiko and Kairi took off, and were half way to Kairi's house when she suddenly stopped and waited until Raiko slowed to a stop as well. Meeting his gaze, she said, "You don't have to bring me all the way back."

Raiko smiled. "I don't mind, and I made a promise. Vaan had no choice to break his, but I won't, unless you truly don't want me around. However, I'll still follow you home to make sure you make it there safely. That is the ninja way, after all."

'Oh shoot, that may have sounded creepy, I'd better say sorry.' Clearing his throat, he began, "I-I'm..."

Kairi started giggling and then laughing as a huge smile filled her face and she took Raiko's hand, leading him towards her home.

~~~~~

After bringing her home, he arrived back at Raven's house where he saw Aurica standing outside. She looked over to him with a smile and he instantly felt happy; running up to her and hugging her tightly. Laughing at his show of affection, Aurica questioned, "How was your day Raiko?"

Raiko had a huge smile on his face, and it wasn't only from being with his sister. "I met some new friends, and... There's this girl, named Kairi..."

Aurica smiled, teasing, "Aren't you a little young for that?"

Raiko blushed brightly, and with a laugh, Aurica softly tapped Raiko on the head and wrapped her arm around his shoulders before they went inside.

~~~~~

Aurica had gone to the academy where she, too, met new friends. The boy from town was there, as well as another loud boy, and a hyperactive girl much like herself. She didn't particularly care for the girl, because even though they were so alike, there were just as many differences. Levi was seemingly happy to see Aurica again, though he didn't say anything to suggest that; but Maize seemed to catch on to his interest, and didn't like that. From then on she didn't like Aurica, and had made it abundantly clear throughout the day. Aurica didn't care though; she knew that staying here meant they'd get stronger so they could save their planet. Nothing else mattered to her. She decided that she would stay in the town for a little while, hopefully being able to become more familiar with the Ariliria and the humans.

~~~~~~

Raiko grew complacent and spent most of his time with his new friends and Raven. He cared about his family, but he just wanted to be a kid and

Aurica encouraged him to be that way. She knew the quest she faced was going to be dangerous, and a large part of her wanted him to stay with Raven and Kim. She made friends too, but always kept her goal in mind. On a cold, starry night, she went for a walk alone, back to the crash site. She looked up, connecting the stars in her mind. Not expecting an answer, she softly questioned, "What? What am I supposed to do?"

"Pardon me, young lady." A young man stood behind her, but he didn't look like one of the villagers. He had silver-grey hair with streaks of green, yellow eyes and was fair skinned.

"Who are you?" she asked, standing tall and strong, refusing to allow him to see her fear.

"Hello Aurica, I'm Sieg, and it's very nice to see you again."

Surprised, she tensed up more. "How do you know my name?"

He smiled and drew closer, kneeling before her. "I'm a dragonoid like you, my princess."

Sieg stood up, waiting for a response, but she was speechless. She looked at him curiously and asked. "Are you here to help? To bring me back?"

"No, my princess, I can't bring you to a place that no longer exists. I'm merely a spectator at this time." He shook his head and said sweetly, before turning his back and walking away, adding, "This is farewell for now."

Confused, she went back to Raven's, thinking of what just happened and what he had said. *'A spectator? What does he mean by that? Is he the one responsible for Azelia's destruction?? No! He was strange, but he didn't have the same feeling as the man who attacked us.'*

She arrived at Raven's late; dinner had already been served, and they were all waiting by the door for her. She apologized and had dinner, wondering what she should do, and how to go about getting stronger. Raven suggested going on missions with the others, and with a nod, she agreed.

~~~~~

She went on many missions with Archer and Levi. Most of the missions were simple escorting, helping to find objects, and the overall welfare of the residents of the village. She learned how people were slowly letting go of the ninja ways; feeling that they were obsolete, and most missions became helping their neighbors. Many of the ninja had left the local villages to join larger armies and to find a use for their skills in the outside world. Before long only Aurica and Calcifer continued doing their training, while Raiko came less and less; his life having become entwined with those of his new friends. Aurica learned to make the most of her new life, all the while planning for her quest and the ultimate mission; saving Azelia.

Part 3

The Time Has Come

ree years passed quickly after their arrival. Aurica; who was about to be fifteen, Raiko; who was nearly twelve, as well as Raven and Kim were finishing up their dinner, which had consisted of pork, broccoli and steamed potatoes. Kim knew that Aurica was planning on leaving, for the girl had become restless, and she made no secret of the fact that she intended on leaving someday. Kim took some of the dishes to the sink; a tear trailing silently down her face when she thought of Aurica and Raiko leaving, as she had started to think of them as her own children. But knowing the heavy responsibilities placed on Aurica, neither she nor Raven would stop her when she decided to leave -- at least that's what they told themselves.

In the dining area Aurica walked over to Raven with heavy eyes, and with a cracking voice, began to say. "Raven... I..."

He stopped her. "I know... But, let's save that until Kim can join us, if that's ok with you."

She nodded as Raiko frowned, but Raven brought everyone back into high spirits and the topic was momentarily forgotten.

Aurica had slipped into the kitchen to help Kim with the dishes, when she saw the tears running down the older woman's face. Kim noticed her and attempted to wipe away her tears, saying dismissively, "Oh, Aurica, I'm sorry. I think it's the onions I cut up before dinner."

Aurica studied her sister-in-law curiously and thought, "*We didn't have onions tonight... Oh!...*" There was a pause, a very long one. "Kim, I'm sorry."

With that she turned around to join Raiko and Raven in the living room, where she found them speaking in low, serious voices. "What are you two conspiring?" she asked.

That brought a smile to their faces, as they knew they looked like they were conspiring. With a mischievous twinkle in his eyes, Raven replied, "Nothing for sisters to know."

When Aurica's smile turned to a disapproving look, they began laughing, which made Kim come out to see what was going on.

Raven decided to be the one to bring up Aurica's plans this time. Exchanging a glance with his wife, he inquired, "Aurica, what were you wanting to tell us at dinner?"

The room went from laughter to silence in an instant. Swallowing the sudden lump in her throat, she answered, "I… I think it's time for us to leave. We're stronger and more capable now, so we should work on finding a way to restore Azelia."

Raiko was looking down at the floor as he carefully considered his sister's words. Watching the boy's reaction out of the corner of his eye, Raven decided to leave the decision to him; there was no changing Aurica's mind, but Raiko clearly wasn't sure about leaving. Aurica saw the look that Raven was giving their younger brother; and knowing Raiko might want to stay, prepared herself for his decision.

"Raiko." Raven said in a strong voice to get his attention. "What do you want to do? Will you join your sister, or will you stay here?"

Aurica spotted the indecision on Raiko's face and stepped toward him. "Raiko, whatever you decide, I shall respect it. I want you to come with me, but I also want you to remain here. The choice is yours."

Relief filled Raiko's face, showing what his choice was without having to say it. Aurica nodded. 'Good. He'll be safer here. Though, being away from him… is going to be difficult. It'll just be Calcifer and me from now on.'

"Very well then." Raven finally said after another long silence. "Aurica, please stay here tonight and we'll pack you a couple of meals."

She nodded and walked closer to her brother, only to see that he was holding in his tears. They had never been separated before, and as far they knew they were the only Azelians left, aside from Sieg. Aurica looked around and spotted Glacey, softly requesting, "Glacey… Protect him."

The dragon nodded as Raiko snuggled closer to his sister, who embraced him as they sat there for a while. Aurica and Raiko eventually fell asleep together on the couch. Raven got a blanket to cover them and went to his room to comfort his wife, as Calcifer and Glacey silently watched over their partners.

The next morning Levi and the others came over to say good bye, while Kim and Raven made breakfast for everyone. Levi tried to convince Aurica to stay awhile longer, but she was determined to start her journey.

Despite them being sad that she was leaving, they laughed the whole time. Levi told her, "You have to come back; otherwise I'll never forgive you."

Aurica smiled and replied. "I promise, I'll be coming back."

Satisfied, he finished his food and thanked Kim and Raven for the meal. Levi reluctantly left with the others, but first he made Aurica pinky promise this time, teasing, "This means you absolutely have to keep your promise!!"

She giggled. "I will, without a doubt!"

They all left, smiling as they talked about Aurica coming back again and what they'd do. Aurica's heart ached as she thought, *I'll come back… but it won't be to stay. I'm sorry Levi…'*

Soon after they left, Kim gave a pack to Aurica. "In the bag you'll find food, clothes, a map, tools, and a water canteen, as well as directions to people who will help you. The people have already been notified and have agreed to help you, so be sure to stop and rest along the way."

"I will." Blinking back tears of gratitude, Aurica placed her hand on her sister-in-law's arm, softly offering, "Thank you Kim… And you too Raven; thank you both so much for everything that you've done for us. Please take care of Raiko and Glacey. I will return from time to time, but right now I have no idea of when that will be."

Turning away from the family she'd grown so close to over the past three years, Aurica began her quest by heading toward a lake along the trail she used to go on with Levi from time to time. She had always felt something weird, yet familiar from it, but since Levi had been with her, she had never investigated. Calcifer felt something this time as well. It was getting stronger, calling out to them; the normally calm surface beginning to ripple. They put their supplies down and prepared to fight, when the waters' current swiftly shifted into a circular motion causing a whirlpool that rose above the surface, drawing the water skyward. Aurica moved closer to examine the phenomenon, while Calcifer stayed behind, wary of the water. She could see a blue stone at the bottom, and it began pulsating; intensifying as she cautiously approached it. She was now standing on the lakes' bottom, looking down at the stone, when she suddenly recognized what it was. There, in a lake in the middle of nowhere, was a water dragon egg!

She knew that Calcifer was waiting impatiently for her to pick it up and get out of the lake; so she gently picked it up and jumped out, holding the egg carefully between her hands as the water began to return to normal. She cautiously turned the egg between her cupped palms, knowing that this was a sign that it was indeed time to start her quest. As the ruler of Azelia, she would have a link to all of the dragons… "That was what Ignis was trying to say before the attack."

She looked down, a single tear trailing down her face and onto the egg, surprising her as it began glowing and moving around. She smiled, hopeful about the new baby dragon about to be born. After several minutes it became clear that it seemed to be having trouble breaking through the shell. She was becoming discouraged when Calcifer put his hand on her shoulder and quietly said, "You have to give it a name, remember?"

Blushing at the reminder, she quietly said, "I name you Anahita… It means 'Goddess of the Waters'." The egg once again began to glow but this time it started cracking as well, and a baby dragon shortly made its way out of the egg. Small and blue, with pink horns and underside, the dragonette blinked blearily up at its queen. As Aurica lifted the newborn up to eye level, Anahita licked her nose and started looking around.

Aurica handled her with one hand as she lifted her pendant to hold it up to Anahita. Anahita bumped it with her nose creating a small blue tear drop shaped addition to her necklace. Since Anahita was too young to turn into her humanoid form, they decided to avoid towns and cities; not to mention if Anahita somehow did transform, she'd be in the form of a baby -- which wouldn't look much better. In a couple of weeks she'd be a toddler and in a month she'd be a small child. She figured that if they did have to stop at a town or city, one of them would stay with Anahita, while the other went in for supplies. Calcifer usually went in for the supplies, as he looked old enough to be on his own, and he didn't like being around when Anahita practiced shooting water.

Together, the three continued their journey with the hope that each day would lead to the discovery of another dragon. Pausing to stare at the horizon, Aurica focused on the barely discernable pulse that only she could feel; the pulse that would lead her to the next dragon. Feeling a stronger pull towards the north, she nodded and turned to her companions with a smile, stating, "This way…"

~~~~~~

Back on Vincent's ship…

Vincent paced as he had been for the past three and a half years. He would lash out at Klaus, but never at Phykira, despite Klaus blaming the whole situation on her. He'd follow Phykira's direction, but it would always lead to a dead end. They occasionally found themselves close to Ariliria, but there was still no sign of Aurica or anyone else they knew. He had traveled to each of the planets in the Azcerek system without being suspected by anyone; in fact they attempted to help him due to his past ties with the royal family. He was careful not to arouse suspicion, and was extremely cunning and quick-witted. Unfortunately for him, however, they had no idea where she was, and were unorganized without their ruler, which disgusted Vincent. He knew Queen Akira was a good person and a wonderful Queen; things had gotten better after she took the throne, but her advisors kept the planning to the Queen and themselves, and didn't allow the other dragons to strategize with them.

Phykira had broken his brainwashing; however, she had acquired a strong distain for her younger sister because of it. She still loved her and didn't want harm to befall her, but she was no longer looking for an escape from Vincent. In fact, her love for him had grown during their time in space. She suddenly felt Aurica's presence one day, a presence that pointed back towards Ariliria, but this time it was clear, strong and there was no doubt about her sister's location. She rushed to tell Vincent; who debated returning to the planet while Klaus scoffed at Phykira, but Vincent believed and trusted her, and they set a course for Ariliria once again.

~~~~~~

Back to the present with Aurica.

It had been six months since Aurica and Calcifer had left the safety of their home with Raven and Kim; travelling northeast, toward another strange pulse of power that they both felt. It grew stronger every day, even when they stayed in abandoned cottages on the outskirts of towns. They both prepared themselves for a fight as the days passed by, always prepared for an unseen enemy to attack. Anahita was growing; getting bigger and stronger every day, and she remained in her original form despite understanding Aurica's pleas for her to learn how to change. She was at the rebellious teenager stage now; using every situation to defy her keepers, and while Calcifer was more of a disciplinarian with Anahita than Aurica, it didn't make a difference. At the end of the day, Anahita defied them equally, much to their exasperation.

After a sudden, violent storm had finally passed, and they were able to leave the cottage they'd sought shelter in before daybreak, Anahita flew ahead, annoying her keepers once more. "Get back here Anahita!!" Aurica shouted.

To make matters worse they saw a figure approaching from the direction the dragon had flown. Anahita realized the danger she found herself in and came back, and as the figure continued toward them, the questors realized that this person was the source of the power they had been sensing. They warily walked down the same path, hoping it was another dragon and not the enemy. It was a young man with dark skin, wearing a short-sleeved shirt that was torn on the sleeves, and knee length shorts that were also a bit torn. He also wore short and thin boxing gloves, his hair was a tad redder than Aurica's and he had a headband pushing his bangs up.

He stopped ten feet away, remaining silent until Aurica was about to speak, when he suddenly offered a slight bow as he inquired, "Well-met, young Dragon Master! What's my name?" Aurica was shocked. She had been called that a couple times before, but none of them had asked for a name, except... *"Wait, I had to name Anahita too! But she was still in an egg, not fully-grown... Does he really not have a name?* The new dragon patiently waited as Calcifer looked at Aurica and whispered, "He had a name until you were chosen, Aurica. Any dragons that were born before you ascended now need new names to signify their bond to you."

She thought of the little she could discern about the new dragon, while the young man continued to wait. "How about..." The dragons' focus had been on her the whole time; but it intensified now.

"What do you think about the name Enki?" She asked softly.

He nodded and jumped back, exclaiming, "Very well then! I am now known as Enki, however before I agree to join you, I wish to test the strength of the new ruler of dragons!!"

Shocked, she had a moment of hesitation, but he was already on the attack. She quickly jumped to her left, but noting the evasion, he quickly changed his direction and went after her.

"Your reaction time is off, but quick thinking... to get your friends out of harm's way!" he shouted.

Pushing aside the surprise his sudden attack had caused, she now had a clear head; staying in a ninja village had helped her adapt to quick and surprise attacks. Clearly she was still not fast enough but she did feel grateful to the village.

Enki frowned as they were punching and blocking, and after several seconds of watching her, growled, "Get your mind focused! You shouldn't be thinking about anything or anyone other than me!"

"He's not even out of breath, and he's so strong! I need help!" Confused as to why Calcifer refused her telepathic pleas, Aurica glared at the dragon as he replied, *"You must do this test on your own. Enki will never respect you if you receive assistance or start to cry during this challenge. Now focus Aurica!!"*

She tried to do as Calcifer suggested, but Enki knocked her to the ground, turned and put his fists on his hips, scowling as he demanded, "Are you *really* the master of dragons? What have you been doing these past four years? Playing around?"

Enki's tone was full of disappointment as Aurica rose to her feet, yelling, "No! I've been training for three years!"

Enki turned his head slightly and retorted, "Could have fooled me, kid. I shall keep the name you have given me, but you are not yet worthy of me. I'll return someday, so be ready next time, as I won't give you a third chance."

Startled by his words, she pleaded, "No, Enki, wait! Give me another chance right now!"

The dragon didn't respond to her plea, clearly ignoring her as he continued to head west, disappearing over the horizon before she could try again. She fell to her knees and tried to hold back her tears, her voice cracking as she whispered, "I failed... My parents and all of our people... I've failed them."

Calcifer stood above her with a comforting hand on her shoulder. "You didn't fail, Aurica; you just need to train more. If you had truly failed, he would have dismissed you completely. And to be honest you do rely on me too much to do the fighting. If you want to stand a chance against our enemies you must become more powerful, and not only fight your own battles, but win them."

Sighing, Aurica swiped at the tears on her cheeks, replying, "I know, but maybe now isn't the time..."

Calcifer shook his head as he interrupted, "Nah, now is the perfect time. You're at your lowest...so now you have no choice but to fight your way back up, and that'll make you mentally stronger at least."

She was silent for a bit, then suddenly rose and patted the dirt off. "Do you think we should head in the same direction as Enki?"

Her partner shook his head again. "No, there aren't any other power signals that way. Enki will come back when he feels like it, just give him some time. In the meantime, *you* should continue to train and look for the other dragons. They aren't all going to challenge you to a fight, but you should be prepared."

She nodded as she turned and walked toward the next power source; one that she could feel humming towards the north. Eyes on the horizon once more, she silently hoped that the next dragon they encountered didn't have the desire to knock her down as well.

~~~~~~

Despite them being the same age, Aurica had always felt like Calcifer was older. He always seemed to know the most random facts about everything, including things that she didn't know existed. She never questioned him because he was always right; at times she thought he might be a reincarnation of an elder based on how wise he was.

Calcifer felt bad for what he had said, but he knew that it needed to be said. He was keeping an eye on Anahita; since Aurica was in a daze, and the small dragon was actually behaving, as if she knew Aurica wasn't in a good mood and felt bad for her. They found a small lake with no one around, and Anahita was told she could splash around for a while. Aurica was focused on trying to find the next dragon, thinking, "*Maybe after I find another dragon, I'll be able to grow stronger...*"

Calcifer could hear her thoughts and wanted to interject, but he had already hurt her after Enki's departure. He knew she'd eventually realize that not only would her plan to wait on another dragon not work, but that she was relying on her dragons too much.

Calcifer left her alone for the time they were at the lake, and despite his dislike of water, he moved to check on Anahita, but Aurica stopped him, softly saying, "I'll go."

He watched her walk toward the lake and dive in, but instead of swimming, she started running laps around the lake, and within seconds Anahita began swimming the laps with her. '*She's figured it out.*' Calcifer thought to himself. When she'd finally exhausted herself, she dragged her body from the water and marched up to him, requesting, "Help me train Calcifer, please."

He nodded with a smile. "I'm ready if you are."

She simply put up her fists and he followed, and they fought while Anahita continued to swim to build up her skills. They trained for an hour, only stopping because Anahita came out of the water and needed to be supervised. Then they had a protein-rich dinner of fresh fish from the lake and called it a night.

In the morning they awoke to a strange man with light skin, light lime-green hair and yellow eyes. He stood silently above Aurica, as they all jumped in surprise. He smiled and bowed. "Good morning young dragon master. I am the wind dragon. Like Enki, the ground dragon, I am looking to you for a name."

She tensed, and at first he was confused, but then his carefree smile came back as he murmured, "I'm not looking for a fight, simply a name."

She relaxed and nodded. "Once I give you a name, what will you do?" She asked in a soft and curious voice. The newcomer tilted his head to the right, answering, "I'm not sure yet. You have two dragons, and that seems to be enough for now. Enki could sense this as well. It's not that you're weak, but that we dragons take your energy. Am I explaining this well young master?"

Nodding, she stated, "Your name, wind dragon, is Aeolus, which means lord of the wind!"

Pondering it for a moment, he agreed. "I accept the name, and I hate to do this to you, my young master, but just as the wind, I must be free... For the time being at least. I will return to you, and when I do, I shall accompany you on your quest. For now, take this." He handed her a tear drop pendant for her necklace. The same as Anahita's, it loosely floated from the crimson crescent moon.

"But this means..." Before she could continue he stopped her. "Yes, it means that I am your wind dragon, but for the mean time I shall watch over you from afar. You'll find the next dragon if you continue to the north. You'll be arriving in a city called Crystal, and I can tell you that the dragon you'll meet there will most likely fight you... but then again, she may not..."

With those words he bowed once more before he turned into a dragon and flew away.

Ana, as they started calling her at her request, walked up to Aurica in her human form. She wore a blue dress, with pink high heels on, and her hair was wavy and light blue just like Aurica's mothers. 'Mother...' Aurica thought after turning around to see Ana. Ana's pink eyes were so beautiful, so unique, and seemed filled with confusion by Aurica's daydreaming. Smiling gently to reassure the young dragon, Aurica offered, "Sorry for ignoring you Ana, thank you."

The three continued to the north towards Crystal. They were currently half-way into Vermillion province, which was the territory Crystal was in. Aurica thought to herself on the way there, "All of the dragons, aside from Anahita, have been in their human form... will they all be like that?"

Unable to provide an answer to her own question, Aurica led her dragons towards the destination they'd been given, too aware that she was racing against the clock to save Azelia, her people, and most of all, her parents...

Water dragons

Ranging from blue and blue-green scales with pink or lavender shell protection for their underside. These dragons are extremely playful, often not realizing they are being a pest. Though they provide Harmony, they tend to become jealous easily. upon reaching maturity they quickly outgrow any rebellious tendencies. They embrace kin (all dragons) above all else.

Water dragon humanoids, ranging blue- green hair and eyes (rarely purple or pink). Ranging skin tones.

Planet name: Luces

Rulers: Kitara and Katrina

Part 4

Decisions

Almost four years ago when the attack on Azelia took place, the citizens that weren't from Azelia fled in a panic as the attack on the castle was taking place. Many dragons and dragonoid people attempted to help Aurica, but they only managed to get in Phykira's way. Two boys; one who was a guard and near Aurica when she was abducted, and the other who was from another royal family, were on the balcony at the time of the attack. They were given access to the balcony because of who they were, but were situated further away, and were among the people who attempted to help but ultimately failed.

The oldest, Conrad, was fourteen and from the Conesteed royal family, as well as Aurica's betrothed. The young guard, named Zander, was only twelve, but had been training to be Aurica's guard for several years. Soon after they joined the fray, two more followed; a girl named Rikku, who happened to be Aurica's best friend, and a boy named Fenris, who was also a guard and junior mentor to Zander. They attacked alongside Conrad and Zander who were trying to determine the best way to rescue Aurica.

Once Calcifer was forced to leave the atmosphere and begin the year long journey to Ariliria, Conrad and Zander tried to leave in pursuit of them, but were stopped by Conrad's father. Zander was able to evade the elder, but Conrad was forced to return home. Zander was joined on his mission by Rikku, who had requested and received Akira's blessing to follow Aurica and Calcifer. They became separated during their journey, but they both continued following the faint trail that Calcifer had left.

Back on Conesteed, Conrad hit the black stone wall of the castle, demanding, "Why did you stop me!"

His father, Ernest, refused to look at him, his face looking as though he wanted to hit the wall too. When the older man remained silent, Conrad clenched his fists in frustration. "Answer me! Now Zander is out there by himself too! We could have already saved her if you hadn't stopped me!" Conrad yelled, his voice echoing through the halls.

"Aurica will be fine. Zander will bring her back safe and sound." After that Ernest walked away, back to his confident, cocky self. Conrad hit the wall again, seething, '*He's keeping something from me! There's no way he'd ever leave things to Zander... Father hates him from everything I've seen.*'

He gave chase, finally locating Ernest in the castles' highest tower. It was an empty room where he'd often go to think, and other than the chair near the window, there were only a pair of Dual swords hanging close by. Conrad closed the door and approached to a certain distance then just stood there, silently waiting for an explanation. It took Ernest a long time to find the needed words, but he finally cleared his throat, saying, "Conrad, what I'm about to tell you is... Is very difficult for me to say. You have to promise to be silent until I'm finished."

Confused, Conrad obeyed; nodding and sitting cross-legged on the floor, patiently waiting for his father to speak.

"You have..." Ernest stopped, putting his hand to his forehead as he fought to get the words out. He turned around, meeting his son's eyes as he blurted, "You have a brother, half-brother to be precise."

Clearly shocked, Conrad's mouth was open as he started to speak, but he stopped himself as Ernest turned back to the window, questioning, "He's two years younger, any idea who he is?"

Conrad had his suspicions, but didn't say anything. '*Zander?*' He wondered. '*No, I doubt even Father would hate his own son that much. Though, why he does is still a mystery.*'

Ernest was second-guessing his decision, but he had already started, and Conrad would never stop asking if he didn't continue. '*Should I really tell him, when maybe a lie will do? No. I've never lied to him, and I'm not going to start now.*'

"Do you know who he is yet?" Ernest suddenly asked, still facing the other way.

Afraid to hear the truth from his father's lips, Conrad was slightly impatient as he stated "No."

Ernest cleared his throat once more, turned around and said, "His name is Zander."

When his eldest son failed to respond, Ernest left Conrad sitting stunned on the floor as he exited the room, glancing at the swords upon the wall as he left.

'No way! Then why?! Why does he hate him so much?! I have to find them more now than ever, Aurica…. Zander… They need me.' Conrad rose to leave, only to see the oldest butler, a dignified man named Virgule, standing in the doorway. The butler bowed, inquiring, "Forgive me Lord Conrad, but did he finish the story?"

Conrad became confused; the condition reflected on his face, as he pondered, 'There's more? Maybe he can explain why dad hates him so much.' Virgule remained in the doorway and began telling Conrad the story of his brother.

After hearing the rest of the tale, he once again found himself sitting on the floor, but this time he felt as though he might throw up. He shakily rose to his feet once more, using the wall for support, and glancing at the Dual swords again before leaving, covered his mouth in disgust as he slipped from the room.

Conrad left Conesteed without speaking to another person, not even his father, who watched him leave from the window in his office. Not bothering to turn around, he addressed the man behind him, his tone tense as he demanded, "Virgule, you told him the rest, didn't you?"

Virgule cleared his throat and nodded, the action reflected in the window glass. "He had the right to know, Sire; Zander does too. Conrad will tell him what he's learned, and when he does, it'll be in Zander's hands to decide your fate."

Ernest stood silently as Virgule gave a brief bow and walked away. 'Good luck my sons. Protect Aurica and bring her back safely…

~~~~~~

Conrad urged his dragon to fly as fast as possible, and on his way out of the solar system he ran into Rikku. She had black hair and orange eyes, and despite her unusual characteristics, she was an electric dragon and Aurica's best friend. She had gone after Aurica and Calcifer, but her dragon had been injured in the explosion of Azelia, which separated her from Zander, and she'd been forced to return to land on a nearby planet. Her dragon had been healed and she was just about to leave when Conrad flew by. She flagged him down; quickly explaining her intentions, and the two of them then left together to find Aurica. Both were silent most of the way, only conversing on their thoughts of where and if Aurica had landed.

Before meeting up with Conrad, Rikku had landed on a planet named Etric so that she and her dragon, Olympus, could be healed. Elefon had arrived just moments before her, and realizing that she was injured, helped her to the castle as the dragon healers cared for Olympus. On Etric the castle was in the center of the most magnetic place on the planet. Magnetic energy ran through the castle so strongly, that even its inhabitants had to be careful when they moved, flew or came in and out of the castle. While Elefon was running madly about, trying to assemble a fleet to find Aurica, Rikku was concentrating as strongly as possible with the racket surrounding her. One thing was immediately clear; Aurica was alive. The new ruler's essence pulsed across the cosmos; pulling at Rikku to join her. The leaders from the other nine planets had come to Etric to lend assistance even though it was dangerous; the dragons of light were furthest away, but were able to arrive almost instantly.

The light dragon leader; a male called Reika, noticed Rikku concentrating on locating Aurica and joined her, quietly questioning, "Rikku of electric, can you feel her? She is closer than we might have thought."

She nodded as she felt Aurica's presence; it was faint, but only because of the distance. She had never been to Ariliria before, but she had been told about its location. Closing her eyes as she thought of searching there, she felt the pull of power grow stronger and suddenly jumped up, exclaiming, "I found her!"

Reika smiled and motioned for the others to gather around her, but Rikku left without saying anything. By the time they noticed that she was gone, it was too late to catch up with her, and none of the remaining dragons knew her well enough to track her as she'd tracked Aurica.

She was happy to feel Aurica's presence, as they all had feared she was dead. She had heard tales of Ariliria and the surrounding planets from Aurica, and as the princess often made doodles of them, Rikku felt that she would recognize them when she came across them. Her dragon Olympus followed the path of heat that Calcifer had left; absorbing the energy into himself so that no one else could follow it. She was relieved when she ran into Conrad on the way there. They recognized Glacey and Calcifer's auras as well, but only faintly. *'If Zander's after her, he'll probably be the first to find her. He and Vincent have always been the best at finding her.'*

After years of travel, in which they were often forced to stop for months in order to rest and strategize, they were finally passing by Jupiter and Olympus was having a difficult time remaining aloft. They had passed many gas giants on their journey, but none as close as the massive planet. Even being aware of its strength didn't help, and Olympus was forced to go out of his way to get away from Jupiter's gravitational field, relaxing only when they made it to a point where the effect was less powerful. As she finally rounded the planet, she saw Mars in the distance, but not Ariliria. Olympus spotted the smaller planet and used his speed to cross the distance to it.

She thought of the first time she'd met Aurica as they flew closer. *'I was sent to the Azelians' castle because I had somehow awakened a strange power. I had always been different, especially with my black hair and eyes. I constantly wondered why I had been born different, so I shut myself off from other people. I met Aurica at the castle, and she didn't look at me strangely and simply accepted me for who I was. She even told me she admired the fact that I didn't care what others thought. She helped me and I helped her. We caused so much trouble for Vincent and the other guards. Aurica stopped caring what everyone thought thanks to me!'*

~~~~~~

They'd believed that Aurica had headed to Ariliria for safety, as it was one of the only planets she had been on for a long period of time before, and as it was a decent sized planet, the chances of the abductor locating her were drastically reduced. Following Calcifer's fading trail of energy, they landed in the same forest Aurica and the others had landed in, before making their way to the town, where they soon spotted Raiko. Ecstatic that their theories had been correct, they ran to him, shouting, "Raiko!!"

Raiko smiled as he met them halfway. He hugged Rikku, as he was one of the few she'd allow to hug her, while Conrad patted his head, teasing, "Still wearing that mask I see. Where is Aurica?"

Raiko looked away, "She… she left to find the other dragons. She gave me the choice of staying or going with her."

They stood silently, surprised by his decision, both figuring, 'He *must* have had a good reason for wanting to stay.'

Raiko quickly laughed. "I would have just slowed her down." Running his hand through his hair, they smiled at him. "There must have been a reason other than that." Conrad stated with a laugh.

Rikku put her hand on Raiko's shoulder and said, "We're happy to know you're both alright. Where is Zander? Is he okay?" Conrad tensed as he looked around, expecting to see his brother lurking in the shadows of one of the buildings. While he hadn't thought that Zander would have stayed with Raiko, he also hadn't expected Raiko to choose to be separated from Aurica. When Raiko shook his head to indicate that he didn't know where the other boy was, Conrad figured he was was either hidden nearby, or with Aurica. Sighing in frustration, he followed behind Rikku and Raiko as the younger boy led them to Raven's apartment house; the latter running up the stairs and bursting inside as he yelled, "Hello Raven, Kim! I'm back!"

Raven and Kim smiled warmly as they turned to greet their charge as he ran into the apartment, the smiles fading to concern as they saw the boy's companions. Quirking an eyebrow as he nodded his head to the newcomers, Raven questioned, "Who are your new friends, brother?"

Nearly bouncing with happiness, Raiko linked arms with Conrad and Rikku, replying, "This is Conrad. He's going to marry Aurica someday… And this is Rikku, Aurica's best friend. They've come to find us!"

Exchanging a glance with his wife, Raven quietly suggested, "Why don't we all have some tea, and you can tell us the story of how you ended up here?"

Nodding wearily after their long journey, Conrad and Rikku happily sat in the chairs offered to them, so fully engrossed in Raiko's tales, that they barely noticed as Kim slipped from the room.

They all remained in the living room talking quietly while Kim prepared tea, happy to have a full house again. Their presence hadn't gone unnoticed, and when some of Aurica's old friends heard that there was a large group at Raven and Kim's home, they immediately went to investigate. A boy hiding in the trees nearby noticed the commotion and followed them, climbing into a tree near the building until he could see in the window. Spotting Conrad, he watched and listened with a relieved look on his face as he learned that the new queen was safe.

Inside they were discussing what they should do about Aurica's absence. Conrad was surprisingly reluctant to look for Aurica, while Rikku was eager to look for her by herself, as she wasn't one for social visits and wanted to leave immediately. Raiko was still unsure if he should go; he had grown stronger, but he had become complacent to his life in the village as well.

Raiko told them about Raven; who he was, and how he had helped them. He told them that Aurica's only thought for the last three and a half years had been of her mission to find the dragons, and how strong she had become. Listening to Raiko's story, Conrad thought of how Aurica must have changed, and without warning Zander came to his mind, followed by his father's story.

He clenched his fist when he thought of the rest of the tale that Virgule had told him. He felt so guilty about what happened, and knew that he had to find Zander; find him, tell him the truth, and hope he would forgive their father. '*I have to find him first… Aurica has Calcifer and any other dragons that she's found; she's well-guarded and I know that she'll be okay.*'

He was so lost in thought that at first he didn't realize that everyone was looking at him with concerned faces. Irritation filled him as he abruptly rose to his feet and announced, "I'm going to find Zander. I have something of great importance that I have to tell him, and it really can't wait any longer.

Aurica has Calcifer with her, so I know she'll be okay." He looked down and softly added, "This is something I have to do."

With a frown, the boy in the tree shimmied down the rough bark and left quickly.

With Conrad and Rikku knowing what they were going to do, they separated; he would find Zander and she would find Aurica. Raiko watched them leave and looked back at Kairi, studying the girl for several seconds before sighing deeply. With sorrow in his voice, he whispered, "I'm sorry."

Not giving her time to respond, he darted towards Raven's house. Kim watched as he stormed in, grabbing his things and quickly packing without saying anything. He shoved the last item into his bag before he looked up at her with a determined expression on his face. "Thank you for everything you've done, but I think it's time I joined my sister."

The words were offered in a happy tone, and with a bitter sweet smile, Kim replied, "If that's the way you feel, make sure to say good bye to Raven."

Offering the woman that had been like a mother to him one last nod, Raiko ran off to find his brother, leaving Kim to wipe her tears away as her heart shattered at the loss of her almost-son…

Part 5

The Bond of Brothers

Thirteen years ago...

Conrad had begun to come over more and more; many of the dark dragons were blacksmiths or were artisans who worked with fire and metal, and he was eager to learn the secrets of metalwork. Conrad used his new-found knowledge to make Aurica a bracelet; a simple one, since she was still a toddler. Though Aurica was walking before she turned two, she still fell down often and usually Phykira or Conrad could be found walking with her. She was walking with Phykira when the older girl became distracted, not noticing that Aurica continued walking without her. By the time Phykira noticed, Aurica was long out of sight. Aurica, realizing that she was totally alone, had stopped and started crying. Vincent was running down the hall, calling her name, and let out a sigh of relief when he saw her. "Princess Aurica, I've finally found you!" He picked the still-crying toddler up and began to walk towards the front of the castle.

They were heading down a long, curved hallway that led out of the castle, when Phykira ran up to them from behind. "Hey, Vincent, you found Aurica! Where are you taking her?"

Vincent turned around at her words, and Phykira thought that he looked aggravated for a moment, but his face instantly morphed into the same expressionless visage he always had. "Princess Phykira, I was taking her outside; would you like to join us?"

She nodded and then suddenly became angry, muttering something under her breath.

Vincent remained calm, his tone soft as he asked, "Is something wrong?"

Phykira nodded again, her annoyance evident as she hissed, "I've told you before you don't need to call me princess."

He smiled. "Is that all? Very well Phykira, my mistake. I won't let it happen again."

As they resumed walking, Vincent continued carrying Aurica, and though she wanted down, she knew that Vincent wouldn't agree, so she remained still in his arms. Phykira looked up at her sister, commenting, "Aurica, I've never seen you stay so still for so long.!"

Vincent laughed under his breath. *'No kidding, I keep forgetting I'm carrying her.'*

Aurica leaned around Vincent to look at Phykira, sticking her tongue out at her before she settled back into Vincent's arms. Vincent smiled at the child's actions as they reached the giant castle door.

"Vincent!" A soldier ran up to him, and seeing that he was carrying Aurica, ordered, "Vincent, please hand Princess Aurica to Princess Phykira and come with me."

Vincent handed Aurica to Phykira and they took off. Phykira looked down at Aurica, and set her down. "Well what do you want to do Aurica?"

Without answering, Aurica ran out the door and onto the balcony, several soldiers immediately following after her. "Princess Aurica? Come back here!"

Phykira laughed and then went after her too, as none of the guards dared to pick her up; instead they just stood by her, trying to convince her to go back inside. But a toddler is still only a baby and they don't listen too well, so Phykira went up to them and they made room for her to pick Aurica up. "Thank you, Princess Phykira, would you like us to escort you back inside?"

She shook her head. "Thank you, but that won't be necessary." They nodded and returned to their posts, leaving the princesses to enjoy the solitude of the balcony.

~*~

The soldier had brought Vincent to where they had observed some sketchy people, only to find that they were gone now, and the men keeping watch on them had been assaulted. Vincent checked on the men down, and after ascertaining that they would recover, turned to the captain, who demanded, "What happened here?"

The soldier who had brought Vincent to the scene quickly explained the situation, to which the captain replied, "I see. I want all of you except for Vincent to go through the castle and the grounds in search of these men. Vincent, you go search the town in case they're hiding there; I'll take care of these soldiers."

They all nodded and left. The captain was a ground dragon, and he made the ground under each of the soldiers lift up in that way carried all of them to the infirmary.

Vincent was well known in the town; it was where he had grown up after all. He asked many people if they had seen any suspicious characters walking around, but no one had. He thanked them and continued on, until he came across a young boy who was playing in the street. The boy had black hair with silver at the tips of his bangs, and simple commoner clothes on.

'That boy, is he a time dragon?' Vincent went up to him and looked around. "Hey there, where are your parents?"

The boy looked up at him and then looked at a house to his right. "They're inside, but they aren't my real parents."

Vincent recognized the house and realized who might still be living there. "Are their names Aria and Micah?"

The boy nodded and stood up. "How do you know them?"

Vincent started walking to the door of the house, replying, "Old acquaintances. By the way, what's your name?"

The boy ran up to him as he reached the door. "I'm Zander, who are you?"

Vincent knocked on the door and turned to answer the boy, when the door suddenly opened. The startled resident of the house demanded, "Vincent? What are you doing here?"

When Micah had opened the door, Zander had hurried to his side. Micah was an electric dragon, with blonde hair and yellow eyes. Nodding at his old acquaintance, Vincent replied, "It's good to see you again Micah. I was in town on business and came across young Zander here. When did you and Aria adopt?"

Zander looked down as sadness filled him and Micah patted him gently on the head, suggesting, "Zander why don't you go inside? I need to talk to Vincent."

Zander nodded and went inside as Micah stepped outside and shut the door. "Let's go somewhere more private." Vincent nodded and followed him; frowning when they went to a lone tree located on a small hill on the outskirts of the town. Micah turned to face him, but continued looking at his hand as he explained, "Zander's mother was dying when we found her. Aria and I were on a walk and saw her carrying him, struggling to remain on her feet. Neither of us are healers, and even if we were, it was too late. We managed to get her to the house and cleaned up, but she died shortly after. It's only been a couple of months and Zander is still deeply wounded... Not that I would expect anything different in this situation."

Vincent looked at the tree, sensing Zander's presence, but chose not to say anything to Micah about the boy's presence, instead saying, "Who knew you could look so down; as long as I've known you, you've never shown sadness over anything."

When Micah didn't reply, Vincent shrugged his shoulders and looked back at him, stating, "I want to take Zander in as my apprentice. He will be trained to be a guard at the castle and given the chance to make something of his life."

Micah smiled and looked back toward the town. "That decision is up to him, old friend. Aria and I will miss him, but I think it'd be a good way for him to cope with his loss and to learn to focus his energy on something productive. I'll talk to Aria about it when we return, and then we can ask him what he wants to do."

Vincent nodded and glanced back at the tree, noting that Zander was gone. 'He already knows how to use his powers. The manifestation must have happened when he lost his mother. I'm impressed, to say the least, as he can't be more than four.' Vincent thought to himself.

They walked back to the house to find Aria and Zander were outside. Zander was playing like he had been when Vincent first saw him, while Aria watched from several feet away. Aria was a wind dragon, with silver hair and green eyes. She looked up at their approach and quickly rose to her feet. Zander noticed the movement, and spotting his adoptive father, stood up as well. Vincent smiled at Aria; glancing down at Zander before turning his attention back to Aria to say, "It's good to see you again Aria, you look as lovely as ever."

Micah hit him on the head and Aria giggled. Shrugging, Vincent defended, "What? It's true, you know… And you look good too, Micah! I never knew you were the jealous type."

Micah hit him again, muttering, "You're pushing it Vincent."

Vincent laughed and Micah joined in, while Aria rolled her eyes and put her hand on Zander's head as the child asked, "Are they friends? I can't tell."

Aria looked down at him and nodded. "We all grew up together. Micah and I have always considered Vincent like a younger brother, but then he went into the castle guard and we hardly ever see him." Vincent and Micah had stopped goofing off at Aria's words, sadness flickering through their eyes as they remembered their childhood.

Aria went up to both of them, closed her eyes as she pointed at their foreheads, poking them right in the middle. Micah's eyes narrowed as he accused, "You cheated Aria; I could feel the wind against my forehead!"

Vincent nodded in agreement. Aria opened her eyes, winked at the men and took two steps back to be by Zander's side again, patting his head as he grabbed her hand. *'Maybe it's still too early to take him away. Aria is a caring woman and he probably thinks of her as his mother now.'* Micah was thinking the same thing, and exchanged a look with Vincent, each noting the concerned look on the other's face.

Aria became confused by their odd behavior. "What's with you two all of a sudden?"

They looked at her and then at each other and laughed again. Irritated, she picked Zander up and went inside while they continued laughing. Vincent was a guard, but he was only fifteen years old and Micah a mere eighteen, so they still found the strangest things amusing. Vincent spent the rest of the day with Micah, and later Aria and Zander; after sending a message to the captain via a passing soldier, informing his commander that he was going to take the rest of the day off. The soldier said that it probably wouldn't be a problem, but he'd tell the captain anyway.

Vincent took Zander aside after they ate. Micah and Aria had already told him that Vincent wanted to take him on as an apprentice, and after giving the boy time to consider what he wanted, Vincent asked, "Have you decided yet, Zander? Its ok if you haven't, as it's a big decision."

Zander was looking down and fiddling with a leaf, and he looked at Vincent. "I'm not sure. I would miss Aria and Micah, and Aria said that after you became a guard, you didn't get to see them a lot."

Vincent put his hand on Zander's head. "Like I said, you don't have to decide right now, and I would make sure that you would get to see them on a regular basis."

Zander didn't say yes, but he didn't say he wouldn't either. Vincent left later in the evening and told Zander that he could visit any time he wanted, as long as Aria or Micah was with him.

A few days later they took him up on the invitation. Vincent was on rounds when he spotted Aria with Zander and ran over to them. Aria smiled, asking, "Hey there, is now a bad time? Zander has been bugging me to bring him to see you."

Zander blushed and hid behind her as Vincent stopped in front of them, a bright smile on his face. "No, now is a great time, as I just finished my rounds. It's good to see you again, Zander."

Zander crept out from behind Aria and nodded. "Vincent, I want to become your apprentice, if you will still take me as one."

Vincent patted his head. "Of course I still want you as my apprentice! I'm glad you've decided to join me, now let's go somewhere to talk."

~*~

Present day...

Zander sat on a tree branch on the edge of town. He had been the one listening in on the conversation and now found himself confused by Conrad's words. *'I wonder what he has to talk to me about... He seemed pretty serious about it, but it better not be about when we were kids. Wait, he couldn't possibly know about that...'* He had been thinking about his past, the parts he could remember. He couldn't remember how his mother had gotten injured, or his mother's face, and every time he tried to picture her he would vaguely see Aria.

When Conrad left the village, he noticed that he was being followed, but he acted naturally and led whoever they were away from the townspeople. The person felt familiar, but he kept his guard up, ready for any attack, until

he was out of the village. There were trees everywhere, with thick foliage; a perfect place for an ambush, but Conrad was confident and strong. He stopped and shouted, "Come on out, enough hiding like a coward!"

Zander jumped out of a tree to Conrad's right, startling Conrad, who had thought he was ready for anything; anything except this. In the back of his mind, he had expected his brother to be with Aurica. Zander waited for him to speak, and after several seconds Conrad managed to compose himself and said. "It's good to see you, though I am surprised to see you here. Didn't you leave before me?"

Zander nodded. "Good to see you, too. Yeah, I did, but I ran into some trouble on the way here, and was delayed in arriving... I was checking up on Raiko, when I saw you and Rikku. I overheard you say that you needed to find me first and speak to me. Why?"

Conrad looked around for a place to talk in private, and after a few minutes of searching, they found a clearing and sat on some fallen trees. Conrad started, "It's going to be hard for me to tell you this, but you have the right to know."

Zander looked confused, but he remained silent and nodded.

Taking a deep breath, Conrad inquired, "Do you remember your mother?"

Zander stood up, anger etched into his face and his fists clenched as he growled, "What does this have to do with her? Don't insult her!"

Conrad remained calm as he replied, "I would never insult someone's mother; I lost mine at a young age, and would never imagine bringing someone's mother into something."

Zander calmed down and sat back down "My mother died when I was young too, and a couple took me in. They told me she had been stabbed, and that she bled to death trying to escape her attacker, all while carrying me in her arms. There is no telling if she would've survived if she hadn't had to carry me away."

Conrad stared down at his hands and struggled to find the words he needed. He was already having second thoughts about telling Zander after the other boy explained his mother's death. He still believed that his brother had the right to know, but maybe now wasn't the right time.

Zander was staring at Conrad with concern. "Are you alright? Was there a point in asking about my mother?"

Conrad looked up and nodded. "It's a long story, and now I'm thinking that maybe I shouldn't tell you yet."

The tension in the air was getting more intense with every moment. Narrowing his eyes, Zander stated, "I'm sure I can handle it, Conrad. You brought it up, so let's talk about it."

Conrad took in a deep breath. "This isn't going to be easy for me to say, or for you to hear… After my mother died, it seemed like my father would never go to another woman. At least that's what I wanted, but he apparently saw someone behind my back. There was one woman who came back into his life, whom he hadn't seen for years; and at first it was mainly comfort that he wanted from her, but that changed. They clearly did something more, because she came back nine months later to tell him that she had a son; his son. She named her son, Zander."

Zander was in shock, but just like Conrad he'd always had a feeling that there was a bond between them, in spite of their apparent animosity towards each other. "Your father told you this? Then he hates me because I'm his son from another woman? Does he know that she died?"

Conrad kept his tone cool as he answered, "Yes he told me, and he doesn't hate you; he wants you to hate him."

"Why does he want me to hate him?" Zander was closer to Conrad now, and nervous about how the younger boy would take the news he was about to give him, Conrad stood and paced several feet away. "See, now this is the hard part. My father made a terrible mistake during one of their meetings; my father was going to ask your mother to marry him; that wasn't the mistake obviously."

Zander cut him off. "How many meetings did they have?"

Conrad became a little annoyed at the interruption, but continued, "They met three times after you were born. The first time; when she came by herself, but the second and third she came with you, at our father's request." He paused. *'I don't want to tell him the rest; he might go after our father in revenge, and the worst part is that dad would probably let him kill him. I'm ashamed that he hurt her so gravely that she died too, but father getting killed wouldn't solve anything, and living with the knowledge he killed her is far worse punishment than just killing him. I'll only tell him the rest if he asks, please Zander don't ask.'*

Zander got up, pacing the clearing in agitation, finally demanding, "Is there anything else?"

Conrad hesitated before he finally nodded. Zander; not liking the expression on his new-found brother's face, turned around and walked toward a large tree, questioning himself, *'Do I want to know the rest, what could it be? Conrad seems hesitant and worried about something. Maybe I shouldn't ask, for now...* He walked back to Conrad, who had his head down in his hands.

Placing his hand on Conrad's shoulder, he waited until the other boy looked up; his weary eyes meeting his own, as he stated, "Whatever it is can wait. Our mission is to find the queen and protect her at all costs... But once we have accomplished our goals, you *will* tell me the secrets you hold, no matter how difficult they may be to hear."

Nodding as he felt the relief of the momentary reprieve flood him, Conrad stood, ordering, "Let's find our queen."

Dark dragons

Their frail and thin scales are a disadvantage, however when these dragons' bond with humanoids, their partners make them armor. Giving each dragon a slightly different appearance. Their scales are always black, the underside of their wings however; range between darker hues. Much like the Time dragons, the Darkness dragons power lie in their tails. They can secrete a glittering mist that disorients their target. They provide industry and progression, they embrace competitive sports/activities.

The Dark humanoids, black hair and eyes, with tinges of blue or red, this would correlate with the dragons' underside color in most cases. Pale skinned.

Planet name: Conesteed

Ruler: Ernest

Part 6

Crystal City and the Electric Dragon

ntinuing their journey brought them to Crystal, the city Aeolus had told them about; and they quickly discovered that it was bigger than all of the small towns they had seen, combined. Almost getting hit by annoyed drivers, they made their way through some of the city, when they were stopped by a police man. "What are you kids doing skipping school? Wait… have you been traveling?" he exclaimed, suddenly going from annoyed to concerned.

They looked down at their clothes, which were worn and very torn. They didn't have much money left and people weren't giving free handouts. The officer began to look around, and seeing no adults with them, took out his phone. Aurica looked at it curiously, while Calcifer looked for a way out without causing a scene; however, it was too late, the once bustling people were standing still, watching and waiting to see what was going to happen. The cop got off the phone and looked at them, especially Aurica who he saw as vulnerable with this older looking boy. "You kids are going to have to come with me."

They did what the man said, knowing that too many people were in the way and staring, that they could only get away by flying, and that was not going to happen.

The cop brought them to a building that said police department on it. They hadn't said anything during the trip to the station, and the cops were beginning to wonder if they could speak. They were brought through the building where many of the operators looked up to see what was going on, and seeing only children, they quickly looked back to their desks and continued working. The other police officers watched as they were brought to the back room. It smelled good; clean, and even though they were being forced, they could tell that everyone there was concerned.

The officers closed the door and prompted them to sit down. He cleared his throat and asked Calcifer, "Where are you kids from? Do you have family here?"

That was only the beginning. In the following hour, he asked so many questions; questions they weren't able to answer, that their heads began to hurt. The interrogation continued until a woman suddenly walked into the room, and approached the officer, who seemed very happy to see her.

"Have they said anything?" she asked with authority. The officer met her gaze with a frown, replying, "No ma'am, I'm beginning to think they're mute, or possibly deaf."

She nodded and looked at them, offering a comforting smile. "My name is Vivian, and you don't need to be afraid, we'll protect you both. Would you both be so kind as to tell me your names?"

Aurica and Calcifer looked at each other and exchanged subtle nods before they looked back at Vivian, who was patiently waiting for their reply. Calcifer noticed that the other officers were treating her with deference, as though she were a higher rank, so he stood up and waited until Aurica did the same. "Ma'am, I'm Calcifer, and this is Aurica."

None of the officers looked surprised that they had finally begun to speak; Vivian was good at getting people to talk about all sorts of things, especially children. Vivian smiled. "What nice names you two have. Could you tell me where you're from Calcifer? Aurica?"

Calcifer nodded. "I can tell you that we've been traveling for a long time; that we left our town almost a year ago, and have been moving Northward ever since."

It wasn't far from the truth, it had been almost a year since they had left Jade village.

She asked them more questions, and eventually someone came in, leaning down to whisper in Vivian's ear. She smiled brightly and looked back at them. "I have been given permission to take you two to my home, if that is okay with you both."

They nodded after a moment, figuring that this option was the best chance they would have at eventually leaving.

Vivian took them to her home, telling her charges that she had some spare clothes that would fit them and make them fit in better to the city life.

"You have some nice kid's clothes; do you have children?" Aurica waited for Vivian's reply, noticing that the older woman tensed a little as she replied; "Yes I do, a boy and a girl."

Vivian smiled with her eyes closed, and then turned around and started working on something. Calcifer came around the corner in the clothes Vivian had provided for him, which were a little big, but other than that, they looked nice on him. He walked over to Aurica who was spacing out. "Hey Aurica? What are you thinking about?"

Blinking her eyes at the intrusion of his voice, she snapped out of it, replying, "I wonder how Raiko is doing, and everyone else, of course. Do you think Phykira is okay? And what about Conrad, he was there, did he get away?"

Calcifer thought for a moment. "I'm sure Raiko is fine. Raven is a good man and your half-brother, and you know that he'll protect Raiko. I'm not sure about Phykira, but she's strong. Certainly Vincent has found her by now… You know he loves her, right?"

She blushed and nodded. She had asked the questions so many times, and while Calcifer wondered about those they'd left behind as well, he always put Aurica first, and he'd never stop. "Believe me, Conrad is fine. He was caught in the chaos, but there is no way he wouldn't be able to escape."

Vivian was listening in, but decided not to ask. Everyone had their own secrets and personal history, and she was very respectful when it came to that. Pretending like she didn't hear anything, she finished what she was doing and turned around. "Now that you're both dressed, you should go to school."

They looked at her confused. Aurica finally said, "We've already studied at a ninja school."

She looked at them, thinking they were joking, but then realized they were serious. "Uuhh, well this won't be a ninja school. Our school is where kids your ages go to learn about this world and other subjects."

This world? That's it! Aurica's hope flared once more as she questioned, "Does school teach us how planets are formed?"

Vivian smiled and nodded. "Yes it does. It really is a fascinating subject, and if you feel like you aren't getting enough information from your classes, I'll see what I can do to fill in the gaps, but you both really should experience school."

When Aurica and Calcifer reluctantly agreed, Vivian was able to pull a few strings to get the two of them admitted into a high school later in its term.

Aurica constantly thought about the formation process, and how to use her current dragons to achieve it, hoping she'd encounter more to help. Her father hadn't taught her very much about planetary evolution, much to her dismay. He'd never thought that she'd have to know about astrophysics, and as she already had so many other studies and practices to attend to, he didn't want to stress her out.

It had been almost a month since they arrived, and though they had stuck out like sore thumbs in the high school at first, they adjusted quickly and took in all they could. They made many friends; despite trying to keep everyone away. They were beginning to acclimate and had begun letting people into their inner circle, as Aurica seemed to need the companionship, and her happiness was the only thing that mattered to Calcifer. He ignored his classmates while Aurica thrived; tolerating their presence for her sake.

Needing open skies around her, Aurica slipped away from Vivian's home and began walking until she reached the outskirts of the city. She didn't like all of the tall buildings that obscured the sky; and walking until she found a small lake, paused to look around. Relaxing as she realized that no one else was around, so she allowed Anahita came out into the open. It was a sunny day; with a few clouds in the sky, and the shimmering lake was of a decent size, with benches around it and a park across the street. Anahita immediately went into the lake, happy to be free and in her element.

When Aurica lay down to take a nap, she looked up and saw a black object in the sky, quickly bolting to her feet and hiding behind a tree. *'That's the ship that attacked Azelia!! ...wait, no it's different.'* *Watching with a frown as* it landed abruptly; sending a massive shock wave out across the water, she was trying to prepare herself for the energy headed towards her, when she felt a presence behind her. Before she could tell who it was, they had picked her up and protected her from the shock wave by wrapping their arms around her. Glancing around the arms obscuring her view, Aurica released a sigh of relief when she noted that Anahita had gone to the bottom of the lake for safety.

Ten men exited the ship; looking dispassionately at the destruction they caused, before talking briefly and dispersing around the lake. Fanning out through the city in search of their quarry, one stayed behind to watch the ship; activating a barrier around the ship that made it invisible to humans. With the ship shielded, it just looked like something extremely large had struck there and had been obliterated by the impact. The man who had protected Aurica released her, and turning around, she saw that it was Sieg. He kept his arm on her shoulder, and without looking at her, said, "I suggest you find a hiding spot, Princess."

Nodding, she hurried away from him and hid in the lake with Anahita. Watching her actions, Sieg vanished with a smirk.

Calcifer had been in the city exploring when the ship landed, and he was spotted by the brothers after jumping onto a roof in an effort to locate Aurica. Now he had nine of the ten men chasing him, and as he jumped from building to building, a voice suddenly demanded, "Where is Aurica? Is she on this planet?"

Calcifer stopped on a roof, an eyebrow quirked in derision as he snarled, "Do you honestly think I'd tell you?"

The men all looked at each other and then back at Calcifer, giving up their chase of him to look for her, as his presence there proved she was on Ariliria. He maintained his position, with the lake she was hiding in in view; he would only move if they got too close.

Aurica was irritated with the fish that lived in the lake; they had fish on Azelia, but they were nothing like the ones surrounding her. A school of them had banded together and started nibbling on her, so she put up a barrier repelling the fish as she stood at the bottom of the lake. *Hmm, that's strange... I feel another presence.*

She looked around at the silt that had been stirred up when she dove to the bottom, and seeing nothing unusual, looked to the surface. She saw the silhouette of a young woman with a parasol; a young woman who stood there as if she was waiting for someone. When the young woman looked up,

Aurica followed her gaze to see the ship leaving, but waited a bit longer, as they were likely still watching for suspicious movement in the area.

Aurica started thinking about what she and Calcifer had learned during their stay. Vivian had been so kind to them, providing a safe place to stay and lending them science and interplanetary books to further their educations. The classes didn't go as in depth as they had hoped, and while you could apparently learn more by going to college, they didn't have time to pursue that avenue. Vivian could tell they were desperate to learn, so she did what she could to help them. With the older woman's assistance, Aurica learned that a chain reaction from a supernova was the likely solution to her mission, and if Calcifer could cause enough heat, it was possible that he could create the chain reaction. She remembered that the research material had said that it took millions of years for the planet to form after the reaction, and that is why having a time dragon was crucial.

Calcifer had studied the book as well, agreeing with her. "Yes it seems that way, but what'll you do if a time dragon doesn't come to you?"

Aurica hadn't thought of it too much, because unless she found an egg of a time dragon, one wasn't likely to come to her.

Calcifer was heading to the lake when he saw the woman, and when she smiled at him, he smiled back. Aurica came to the surface and saw them staring at each other, seemingly oblivious to her presence. They both looked at her as she cleared her throat, raising an eyebrow as she crossed to stand beside Calcifer.

"You're a electric dragon, aren't you?" she inquired in a strong tone. *'Aeolus said she'd fight me, but she doesn't look like a fighter, she's beautiful.'*

The new dragon nodded and stated. "I am, though I will require a new name, after you prove yourself, of course. You aren't off to a great start, as hundreds of innocent people just died while you hid in a lake."

Aurica clenched her fists as anger flooded her, looking down to keep from attacking the dragon. The woman began laughing, and Aurica's head jerked up; her eyes flashing dangerously, but she knew the other woman was right, and at a loss for words, Aurica stood still.

Calcifer put his hand on her shoulder, squeezing gently as he softly said, "Aurica, look up at the city."

She slowly did; knowing that she'd have to accept it at some point, her eyes going from sad to shock and joy in an instant. The city was whole again!

The electric dragon looked back at it in surprise, but she, too, was happy. Unbeknownst to the group, a figure in a gray suit and silver hair watched from a distance. After looking around and then back to Aurica's group, he vanished.

"They'll tell their boss you are here; we should stay alert." Calcifer said breaking the silence.

Aurica nodded, and they turned to walk back to the city when the electric dragon drew their attention back to her. "So Princess, do you not want me on your team?"

Aurica turned around with a smile. "I do, but first I want to investigate the city. I felt the presence of another dragon element, one I've never sensed before."

Aurica and Calcifer went back into the city, leaving the other dragon behind. The electric dragon sensed a presence behind her; one quickly followed by a deep voice. "What an interesting princess."

She nodded, turning to face him, bluntly asking, "Did you have anything to do with the city returning to normal?"

He shook his head and replied, "No, that wasn't me, but I do know who did it. He has been making it difficult for her enemies to find her, but now they are here, and you will need to decide your fate. Join her, or join me."

She smirked and looked away. "You already know my answer."

He carelessly shrugged and vanished into thin air, leaving the electric dragon standing alone.

She remembered when she had first changed from a full-fledged dragon into a Halfling...

'I remember it so well. I was so shocked by what had happened to me and actually a little angry. My life as I knew it was over, or so I thought when it happened. I immediately set out for Etric, where my best friend, Elefon, lived. He's the current King of Etric, and though I hadn't seen him for a while, I knew that if anyone could tell me what had happened, it'd be him. When I first saw him, he didn't recognize me until I got so frustrated that I changed back to my dragon form.... In the castle... He still hasn't let me live that down. He was completely stunned and began to lead me to Azelia, of all places. But, oh no, it didn't end there, for he led me inside the castle. I followed close behind looking at the mesmerizing crimson interior and lava; yes lava, in ducts going horizontally throughout the castle. I must have been so fascinated because I bumped into

Elefon when he suddenly stopped. That ticked me off until I noticed him bowing to two figures ahead of him. I immediately stopped beside him and bowed as well, because for all I knew, we had met the Queen in the hall. I reluctantly looked up and saw Jeticous; the King, and first princess Phykira, smiling and motioning for me to look up all the way.

I greeted them, but I don't remember much from that moment. After that awkward introduction, I was led to Queen Akira's private room, where we saw her holding a baby close to her, with a small fire dragon curled up next to them. She greeted us and then focused on me. 'Okay, it's time,' I thought. 'I'll tell her what happened, and since Elefon brought me to see her in person, I guess that she will have the answers I need'.

I was about to speak, when Elefon asked to see the baby. I couldn't believe it! We were there for me, yet he was just trying to get a sneak peak of the new princess! He thanked her, carefully took the princess into his arms, and then turned around to show me the baby. That's when it happened. Once I looked into her big, crimson eyes, I knew that my life would never be the same again. Everyone else could see that something had happened, but Elefon just smiled and handed her back to her mother. I left that night, knowing that I should do the things I wanted to do while she was under her parents' protection and much too young to have more than one dragon. I think we forged the bond then, because I heard that the princess changed after that, too. She began asking about electric dragons as soon as she was able to talk, and now the time has come. She needs me, but after my comment, I'm sure she'll want to fight to prove herself...'

Not realizing that the being that had restored the city was watching as she pulled herself from her thoughts, she pasted a smile onto her face and ran off to find Aurica, calling, "Time to find the princess!"

Watching as the electric dragon faded from view, the mysterious newcomer taunted, "It appears that she has chosen the princess over you."

Sieg came out from behind a tree and shrugged. "Indeed, but I was never counting on her. Aurica is a compelling person without trying, and some find themselves drawn to the new queen without even realizing it. I do wonder about your intentions though, as you haven't been swayed either way, or so you want me to believe. I know that you've been assisting her from the shadows, and that you restored the city. Now, was that because you felt bad for them, or did you wish to make her happy?"

The man turned away, ignoring the question and focusing on the city.

After several minutes Sieg gave up on receiving an answer and stated, "I'm sure you know, but things only get worse from here. Not only for her, but for the humans if she stays. You can't protect her from everything, so what makes you so protective of her? Surely the great Horus isn't attached to a Halfling brat!"

Horus turned towards Sieg, and with the same expressionless face, replied, "You're right, I didn't intend to baby her, however, don't act like you don't know why I do so. She isn't just some brat; there's something powerful and unwavering about her, I'm just not sure what." *'Am I overprotective? I have never felt this way, the only thing that's been on my mind for the past 16 years is her, ever since I saw her that day.'*

With a brief flashback to a crimson castle and a newborn baby girl with crimson eyes, he remembered feeling strange; compelled to protect the infant, and hadn't been able to forget her. He, too, had been a full-fledged dragon, and had never thought he'd be destined for another, but his entire future had changed that day.

Shaking his head to clear the memory, Horus turned until he was again facing the city, completely ignoring his fellow dragon. Sieg sighed and vanished, after which Horus walked toward the city to continue to watch over Aurica. He found her strolling through the city with a smile on her face. *'So innocent and naive... I thought my point in living was gone, however, you have given me a new purpose and reason for living, little queen...'*

He watched as she wandered through the city, crossing many of the urban streets until finally locating her quarry; the electric dragon. *'The electric dragon... She intends to join Aurica, so her power should be enough of an advantage for the queen to avoid a dangerous and deadly fate... Farewell for now, Aurica.'*

~~~~~~

The electric dragon was in a new outfit; a purple tunic, with black leggings, a belt, and a grey cardigan. She stood tall before Aurica and asked, "Well, are you ready to decide?"

Aurica smiled and nodded. "Electric dragon! I-"

She was stopped by the lighting dragon. "First a name. My old name was Jazlynn, however; as I'm sure you're aware, I need a new name to signify our bond. So, Princess Aurica, what have you decided?"

Aurica nodded and took a deep breath. "Your old name was beautiful, so I hope you like this one. Damini is the name I choose."

The dragon stood with her head down for several long seconds before she smiled and slowly raised her head to meet Aurica's curious eyes. "Accepted!" she proudly declared, secretly loving the new name and the meaning behind it.

'That'll surely strengthen our bond, right?' They both thought, sharing the same concern over what the other felt about them.

"What's your next move Princess?" Damini asked in a soft tone.

Surprised by her sudden change in attitude, Aurica tried to choose her words carefully so as to not lose the respect she had just earned. "I know the Wind dragon, Aeolus, will come to us eventually; as will Enki, so I was thinking of heading west. I keep sensing something strange out that way."

Damini nodded, knowing what she was sensing. "Very well, though… Would you like to watch my showcase before we go? I'd appreciate it…"

Aurica nodded, feeling giddy and excited for Damini's sudden change of character. 'Hopefully Aeolus and Enki will join us soon. I have a bad feeling, and though Damini has come to my side, I sense she's hiding something...'

~~~~~~

Damini's showcase was exciting, and she even pulled a couple of strings to get Aurica into the show, both of them startling the audience. Sieg was there, and when he made eye contact with her, Damini winked at him, prompting a smirk and wink back. She then noticed a man sitting next to him and narrowed her eyes as she studied Sieg's companion. He's a dragon too. Oh boy, Aurica, I don't know about Sieg or this new guy, but I will protect you.

The men left before the end of the show, passing Rikku, Raiko, Conrad and Zander on their way out. The four of them quickly found Calcifer, who then led them to Aurica. She saw Raiko first, and seeing his sister, Raiko ran past the others, tackling Aurica. Giggling happily, she barely managed to shift her weight so that they'd spin rather than fall, exclaiming, "Raiko why are you here? I'm happy to see you whatever your reason is! I was…" Stopping herself, she hugged him tight again, whispering, "Never mind the reason, I'm so happy that you're here!"

They both teared up as they examined each other. The others waited as patiently as they could until she finally noticed them, hugging each of them in turn. Conrad was still hugging Aurica as he murmured, "You know I don't want to let you go, right? The last time I saw you, I couldn't help you, but I'm not leaving your side ever again."

He did eventually let her go. "I'm so happy you're all okay, I was so worried about all of you!! I didn't know whether all of you had made it off of Azelia safely, or what had happened to you."

They all grouped together and hugged, Aurica quickly reassuring them that everything was going to be okay, but prompted concern in the others when she announced, "I have located three of the dragons."

"It hasn't been that long, Aurica, so you should take it easy. We passed through many of the places you went through, and it seems you've been very busy." Zander said, the others nodding in agreement. She shrugged and smiled her biggest smile since the disaster had happened, and they all relaxed knowing that she was too stubborn to stop. They all left Crystal, heading west towards Agate town. Aurica felt a familiar dragon presence, but couldn't pinpoint it, silently pondering….. 'Phykira?'

They came across a river that drained into a collapsed limestone cavern; marveling at its beauty from afar, before they headed south to go around it, when they saw someone down in the cavern. The person stood up and jumped out of the hole, startling them. Their concerns eased when they realized that it was Enki. He greeted Aurica, seemingly ignoring the others. Calcifer put his arm out to keep the others behind him, as Aurica walked toward Enki, knowing that a fight was about to ensue.

Aurica had more agility and a good amount of strength, and while Enki was slower, he was much stronger. He couldn't land a single hit on her, but when he rushed by her, she was happy it didn't connect. She hit him with multiple fire blasts; which hurt him, but didn't slow him down. After about ten minutes Enki stopped, stating, "You have proven yourself. You clearly have speed, but you require more strength; I shall be that strength. I accept the name that you have given me, and now I give my power to you."

Nearly out of breath, Aurica sighed with relief at his words. They walked toward each other and Enki knelt as Damini had, waiting as Aurica placed her hand on his forehead. A light enveloped both of them, and for a brief moment Aurica's red eyes turned brown. As her eyes returned to normal, a glowing, reddish-brown orb came out of him and turned into a teardrop on her necklace.

Zander walked over to her "Aurica? How do you feel?"

Aurica smiled brightly, replying, "I'm fine Zander, absolutely fine."

They camped out that night and Enki remained with them. He got along best with Calcifer, but he enjoyed Anahita's company more. Aurica was very tired from everything that she'd experienced, but refused to show it; the last thing she wanted was to lose Enki's respect. Enki slowly loosened up as the evening passed, eventually coming over to sit by Aurica. "You should get some rest… I know my power, and it's going to hit you hard if you don't take it easy."

She looked at him and nodded. Calcifer walked back to Aurica, sitting beside her and pulling her close to keep her warm. Anahita and Enki went inside the tent, and Zander moved over to Aurica's other side.

At daybreak, they all set out again, noticing that it was getting colder and that the trees were losing their leaves and were beginning to turn different colors. All of the dragons decided to come out and walk with them. For most of the day, Aurica conversed with Enki, stopping for sparring sessions every now and then. Enki had a lot of respect for Aurica, and he was happy that she was trying to get to know him better. Calcifer joined them in conversation several times, while Zander sparred with Conrad. Zander's dragon revealed himself, but didn't do anything, just sat with Rikku, who was practicing her powers.

Aurica looked over at Zander's dragon, realizing that she had only seen him a couple of times over the years, and each time he had just lain in one spot. Frowning, she called, "Zander your dragons name is Saros, right?"

Zander nodded, not volunteering any other information, but noted that his dragon was looking at them now. Saros was a dark gray; which could classify it as a dark dragon, but there was something; very off about him; something that made Aurica cautious around the dragon. Zander kept his secrets close, never revealing exactly what he and Saros were. Aurica rested as everyone kept suggesting, surreptitiously studying Zander and Saros as she wondered where the gray dragon and his humanoid fit into her quest.

Electric dragons

They're serpent like in appearance with long electrified tentacles coming from the sides of their heads. Next to and above the tentacles are multiple spiked horns, the wings were large and long with spiked horns at the end of them. The color of the electric dragons was always a lime yellow with a dull blue being the color of the tentacles and under guard. They continually release electricity, making most approaches difficult. They seem hard to tame but they prefer companionship over isolation. They provide order and protection and they embrace rules.

The electric humanoids, ranging blonde hair, deep yellow eyes with tinges of green or blue, ranging skin tones.

Planet name: Etric

Ruler: Elefon

Part 7

Kairi Brings Aquilo, the Dragon of Ice

Kairi left school early and saw the tree that she had sat under with Raiko; blushing and immediately running to a field that was normally very warm, but was now as cold as ice. Realizing that she was not alone, she slowly approached the male figure that had appeared, shocked to find that he looked like Raiko! He turned around after hearing the nervous girl's footsteps; sighing in annoyance before he turned back around.

Irritated by his attitude, Kairi still approached him, about to ask him a question, when he softly asked, "Do you know a girl named Aurica?"

He was peering over his shoulder, waiting for a response, so she simply nodded. He turned around, completely facing her now, as he demanded, "Do you know where she is?"

The man noticed her shivering, and with a sigh took off his coat and handed it to her. She accepted it, welcoming the warmth as she answered, "I know that she was heading north, but that was several months ago."

As he grunted under his breath, Kairi realized that he was just a teenager, about the same age as Aurica. He thanked her and began to head north, when Kairi ran after him; pulling at him until he stopped once more, pleading, "Please! Allow me to come with you!"

After a moment, he finally spoke. "It may become dangerous, even for a Halfling."

She ignored the last part, and quickly said, "That's okay."

He gave her a quick nod. "Meet me outside your town in two hours. Be there, because I will leave; with or without you."

She nodded with a smile and he turned away and headed north once more.

Kairi rushed back to Raven's house to tell him the news. In all that time with him, they had grown close through their relationships with Raiko. That's exactly why she had to go; finding Aurica made any danger worth it, especially since she'd be able to see Raiko again. Raven was outside when he saw her running over to him. "Raven, I must leave and find Aurica. I found someone who is looking for her and he looks like Raiko!!!"

Raven looked around for said person and seeing no one accompanying the young girl, admonished, "You can't up and leave with some random person Kairi! That's dangerous!"

Kairi looked at him with disapproval, making him annoyed. Throwing her shoulders back defiantly, she declared, "I'm going with him! He shouldn't travel alone."

Her response surprised Raven, and with sadness in his tone, he said, "You aren't going to listen to reason, are you?"

Shaking her head, Kairi turned and began running towards home, aware of the time slipping away from her and fearful that the man would leave without her.

Kairi somehow got permission to leave, although it didn't take much to get her guardians to agree; they had always wanted her to get out there and see the world, but without being on a dangerous mission. Her instructor wasn't pleased, but as her guardians had given her permission to go, she couldn't keep Kairi there, despite not knowing who this person was. All her guardians heard was that she was leaving with a boy, and then name Raiko was mentioned, who they knew, so they saw no problem with it. The guardians were two men; one was her father and the other was his husband, and while she'd often asked when she was younger, her father had never told Kairi anything about her mother. He did care for Kairi more than anyone else, and despite letting her go so easily, he loved her and wanted her to experience the world.

Kairi met up with the mysterious youth and they set off in what she knew was the general direction Aurica had intended on going, with the boy acting as though it wasn't going to be that hard for him to find her. Slightly irritated by his attitude, Kairi questioned, "Oh, right, what's your name?"

He stopped and frowned before he stated, "My name? It doesn't matter. That will change when we meet up with Aurica."

Without giving her time to react, he continued walking. He was determined to find Aurica, and as they passed through each town he believed that she must have traveled through, they talked to a several people as they shopped for supplies. Some of the people from the towns were worried about them traveling alone, but they slipped away before the townspeople could do anything to stop them. They came to a city called Crystal, and he looked around in fascination. "Kairi, what's this place called?"

Kairi shook her head. "I'm not sure, as I've never been this far out. I think it's called Crystal City, but I could be wrong."

His fascination subsided quickly as he picked up a powerful presence. Kairi was skipping ahead while he was walking behind her, looking side from side as he could sense the presence more now, realizing that it was heading towards them. It was the mysterious man called Horus. The man remained expressionless as they approached him, but he kept Kairi behind him just in case.

"You, too, have been changed." Horus blankly stated, barely making any gestures that would suggest his intentions. The young man nodded as Kairi peered around him, trying to figure out what they were talking about, when Horus suddenly turned away, pointing southwest as he added, "Aurica is heading that way now, and she may be in danger so get a move on."

Horus began walking away and then suddenly vanished before their eyes. The young man changed their direction of travel towards the southwest, but he seemed unsure to Kairi. "What's wrong? Do you think he was telling the truth?"

He looked back at her and nodded. "Say, Kairi? Have you ever seen a dragon?"

Perplexed she shook her head, and he sighed at her response. "Aurica and Raiko mentioned dragons a lot though, now that you mention it. To tell the truth I don't even know the real reason they left. Why, is Aurica is danger?"

He put his hand to his chin. *'She really doesn't know? Even though she is like those two... I can't worry about that now. He did tell me to hurry, so I guess I have no choice.*

Meeting her eyes, he said, "You're eventually going to find out, one way or another, so just promise not to freak out."

Not giving her time to question him, he reached for his true self, and allowed the change to wash over him. Confusion and awe filled her and was reflected on her face as she watched him transform into a blue-gray dragon that had five horns; the longest of which went up and drew close to the neck at times of flight. The next four flanked the first, getting smaller as they got further away. The mouth had a more pronounced peak making it easier for ice dragons to dive into thin and medium sheets of ice, and he had spikes running down the outer sides of the front legs and an extra claw on the hind leg feet for gripping. His wings constantly had a thick chilling air around them, making her shiver.

He made a path for her to climb onto his back; protecting her from his subzero scales, extremely surprised that she didn't hesitate as much as he had feared. They had bonded; she trusted him, and she feared for Aurica and Raiko. They flew in the direction Horus had pointed, quickly finding Aurica and the others.

"Raiko!!! Hey, look up!" Kairi shouted with excitement.

Raiko and the others looked up, and spotting the dragon, immediately looked around to make sure no one else was in the vicinity. Raiko suddenly caught his breath and exclaimed, "Look, it's Kairi, and she's riding on an ice dragon!"

Aurica smiled and waved them down, the dragon barely landing before Kairi jumped off of him and immediately ran to Raiko. The ice dragon turned into his human form and walked over to Aurica, who was watching Raiko and Kairi. *My brother, you have found someone who will do anything for you despite the obstacles, she truly does love you. So why am I so hesitant?*

"Aurica?" he inquired, standing just three feet from her. He asked the question with no emotion on his expressionless face, but she was getting used to the dragons that had been born before her acting this way around her. She turned to face him and smiled. "Hello ice dragon, may I ask your name?"

Even if he wanted to fight, she had the advantage, and he knew that too. But even with that knowledge, he never had any intentions of fighting her.

He shrugged. "I don't think that would make much of a difference. I am here to join you, and will be given a new name by you."

She smiled and stated. "I would be more than happy to give you a new name, but it's important to respect your past. Please, allow me to know your present name."

"Very well. My name is Grey, and I was hatched around the same time you were born." He bluntly said, still showing no emotion.

"I see. Then I give you the name of Aquilo." He nodded, adding his power to her pendant. He walked over to Raiko and Kairi who were talking about what had happened since they last saw each other.

"Thank you for accompanying me, Kairi." He offered the words with a smile and then turned to Raiko. "You must be Raiko. I have heard a great deal about you from Kairi."

Raiko nodded with a smile. "Well met, dragon. Thank you for bringing Kairi with you, and for keeping her safe. Hopefully she told you nothing embarrassing..."

He shook his head. "No nothing like that. Hmmm..." He turned back to Kairi, adding, "By the way Kairi, I am now known as Aquilo."

Offering her hand, she gave him a firm handshake, stating, "A name at last."

A wry smile flickered at the corners of Aquilo's mouth as he replied, "Indeed."

~~~~~~

It had been a week since Kairi brought Aquilo to Aurica. Aurica was so happy to have everyone there; especially Raiko, whom she had missed terribly, and was happy to see that he was much stronger now. She enjoyed having Kairi there too. Even still, Raiko expressed interest in taking Kairi back, saying he felt she shouldn't be put in any further danger after hearing what the mysterious man she had confronted earlier had said. Raiko dreaded leaving Aurica, and she did too, as they had just been reunited.

Zander was getting ready to go get some wood for the fire, when Raiko and Aquilo asked if they could come help him. Zander was more than happy to have them assist him, as gathering firewood was a boring job. Kairi stayed with Aurica at the camp and helped her prepare a meal. Aurica wasn't very good at cooking, but Zander never complained. Kairi was good at it, so she helped.

"It's great having both of you here," Aurica said, smiling down at Kairi.

Quickly hugging the other girl, Kairi replied, "I'm happy to be here."

The meal was simple; just some mushrooms and other edibles they'd found in the forest, and as they worked, Aurica and Kairi bonded quickly. While they had little in common in both appearance and interests, they still got along quite well. As the girls prepared the meal, Conrad spent his time talking to Calcifer and Enki, while Anahita, Damini, and Rikku; who had quickly bonded, left to investigate the sinkhole, saying they'd felt a strange presence coming from there.

As she mixed nuts and herbs in with the mushrooms, Aurica glanced around at her companions and smiled. If only her mother could see her now...

Ice dragons

They are medium in size but not spirit, they are fierce when provoked even challenging fire dragons. They range in blue-gray tones, very rarely blueish green. They have pronounced peaks allowing them to dive into thin and medium sheets of ice. They have spikes running down the outer sides of the front legs and an extra claw on their hind leg feet for gripping. Their wings constantly have a thick chilling air around them. They provide innovation and embrace acceptance and unpredictability

The Ice humanoids, blueish grey hair, pale – steel blue eyes, pale skinned.

Planet name: Nieve

Rulers: Ysuelt and Frost

The Queen's Memories Part 1

'*Aurica is now two, and I'm pregnant again. I so hope it's a boy!!!*' Akira wrote in her diary as she smiled with excitment. Aurica was sneaking around behind Akira, while Calcifer watched from the ceiling. Akira knew Aurica too well, and as the little dragon jumped into the air and came at her mother from the right like she always did, Akira caught Aurica in midair, bringing her close and hugging her.

"How'd you know??" Aurica asked while giggling.

"I'm your mother; I just know these things, my darling," Akira replied softly.

Jet walked in with Phykira trailing him. The older princess was now twelve, and really loved her stepfather. She didn't want him to leave, and while Jet sometimes became aggravated by her constantly following him, he understood why she did it.

Aurica wiggled out of Akira's arms and ran towards Jet, but passed him to run to Phykira, who twirled so that she didn't lose her balance. Laughing, Phykira said, "Someone sure is hyper today!"

Aurica just leeched onto her sister and nodded, but then suddenly slid off of Phykira to tackle Jet; who wasn't ready for her and they both nearly hit the floor. Steadying himself, Jet turned around and agreed with Phykira, before bending to pick up Aurica, who was on the ground laughing. They made their way to Akira, and as Jet stopped before her, he said, "You look so sad, my love. What's wrong?"

Akira gave a little laugh, replying, "Oh, I'm not sad at all! I'm happy and... Well, kind of worried."

The only thing Jet managed to catch was that she was worried. Moving closer to his wife, Jet demanded, "What's the matter? Is something wrong with you or..."

Cutting off his words as he realized their children were still present, he turned to glance at Phykira, and then down at Aurica, relieved to see that she had fallen asleep in his arms.

Akira stepped closer to him and put her hand on his face, whispering, "Everyone is just fine, Jeticous, of that I can assure you. The thing is... I'm pregnant again!"

Jet's eyes widened in surprise and he moved to hug her, only to realize that he still held his daughter. Turning to the side, he asked Phykira if she could take Aurica for a bit, and after the hand off, Jet wrapped his arms around Akira and gently kissed her on the lips. Turning away from their display of affection, Phykira was surprised to find how light Aurica was. She hadn't been allowed to hold the infant often; always being told that the baby was too fragile.

Jet and Akira watched their two daughters, noting the protectiveness that Phykira displayed towards the toddler in her arms, happy that they were getting along. Now that they were having another child, Akira was worried that she would have another hyperactive kid, and she wasn't looking forward to that possibility to say the least. She knew that this would be her last child, and when their youngest was eight years old, Ignis would decide which child would be the new ruler.

Phykira watched Akira, knowing that this was the real reason that her mother was worried. It'd always been so hard being the oldest, and knowing that one of her younger siblings might be more suited to taking the throne than she was. Even though she had more experience, she had her doubts about her ability to rule Azelia, and thus never attempted anything that might change the future. The fact that Aurica had been born with a rare fire dragon; and more than likely would be chosen as the next ruler unless the girl had bad intentions deep within her heart, had never inspired any confidence in Phykira that she would be the next queen. Despite the fact they lived on the fire dragon planet, fire dragons were scarce after the war, which had nearly destroyed Azelia. The war had damaged the planet, making it fragile, and requiring Ignis to remain there for the rest of his life to maintain and rebuild the balance. Ignis had quickly learned that he needed a compatible dragon-humanoid to assist with the massive burden on the fragile and explosive planet, and the bond between the fire dragon and the ruler of Azelia had been born.

Pushing the deep thoughts from her mind, Phykira glanced down to find that Aurica showed no signs of waking any time soon. Turning, Phykira started walking towards the door with her sister soundly asleep in her arms, thinking that the younger girl would sleep better in her own bed. After kissing Akira, and saying that he was going to make sure Phykira got Aurica to her room safely, Jet followed after them. Jet and Phykira were walking toward Aurica's room when they heard a loud noise and paused. Realizing that the disturbance was coming from the training hall, Jet gave into his curiosity, and asking Phykira to follow him, started in that direction. Casting his gaze at the young woman, he softly told her to hand Aurica to him if she became tired of holding her.

Smiling, Phykira continued to follow Jet as she replied, "I'm fine. She really doesn't weigh that much."

Nodding at her words, they entered the hall and saw that Conrad was there, sparing with a young man that Jet had never seen before. Vincent was watching from several feet away, glancing in the direction of Jet and the princesses as he sensed their arrival. He rose and waited for them to descend the stairs, and seeing Aurica in Phykira's arms, said, "This really isn't a place for the youngest princess."

Jet nodded and told Phykira to remain there, walking over to Conrad and Zander, who had stopped when the royal family entered the hall. Zander was panting, but gathered the strength to bow and greet the king properly. Jet returned the greeting, and asked who he was. The young man's back straightened and he replied, "I am Zander, sir! I'm five, and I am Vincent's apprentice".

Conrad bowed and greeted the King, before walking over to Phykira, Vincent and Aurica. He looked at Aurica and asked, "How long has she been asleep"?

Phykira glanced at him and replied, "Less than an hour. We were on our way to her room when we heard noises coming from here."

He laughed and said, "Yes, sorry about that, but that fool over there is weak! Luckily for Aurica, she won't need him as a body guard, as she has me!"

Zander heard the declaration as he and the king walked over, and clenching his fists, countered, "I may have a lot of training to do, but I am not weak!"

Conrad smirked and crossed the room to train some more. Zander walked over to look at the sleeping princess, promising, "Don't worry, Princess, I will protect you, and I'll get stronger."

Nodding to the king, he ran off to go train again, leaving Jet smiling and shaking his head as he said, "Oh great, she already has boys fighting over her!

Phykira laughed and said goodbye to Vincent, before she and Jet left the training hall. They chatted quietly on the way to the royal bedchambers, finally arriving at Aurica's room, only to have her awaken as her sister moved towards the bed. The younger girl jumped out of Phykira's arms and stretched, before casting a coy look up at her sister and giggling.

Phykira was ready to hit her for making her carry her all that way for nothing, but the King held onto Phykira to make sure she didn't hurt Aurica. Chuckling at his daughter's antics, Jet turned as he heard footsteps stop at the door, and as he walked over to the portal, someone started knocking. Jet opened the door to find Conrad and his father standing there. His father greeted Jet first, as he knew Jet had been in the war on Ariliria, and had some respect for him. As the men sized each other up, Conrad saw that Aurica was now awake and went over to her. He was eight, and very strong, so he was able to pick her up easily, and she wanted him to because he always spun her around, but he didn't do that this time because his father was there. Aurica was bummed, but didn't say anything because she was afraid of Conrad's father.

Conrad's father walked up to Jet and said, "Good day, King Jeticous! I don't think we've ever been properly introduced. I am Lord Ernest."

Jet smiled and replied, "Lord Ernest, it's a pleasure to finally meet you."

Ernest nodded in agreement and turned to Conrad and Aurica, stating, "Well, it seems that you two get along just fine. That's good to know, as I was worried about the age difference and all, but this seems to work."

Conrad looked down at Aurica and replied, "Why would age difference matter? This way, she can grow up, and I can still fight and not have to worry too much about her."

Jet clinched his fist a bit, but no one seemed to notice. He didn't like how

Conrad was always fighting, and Lord Ernest only encouraged him to do just that. Ernest's wife had died shortly after Conrad was born, and though Ernest had truly loved her, he had never showed it. He had refused to remarry, but had never told Conrad the reason. Conrad believed that it was because his father just didn't want another person to have to worry about.

When Aurica suddenly yawned and snuggled into Conrad's chest, Ernest's expression became sad, but Conrad didn't notice, and even if he had, he wouldn't have understood why.

Jet noticed and decided it was best to go somewhere else to talk, and leave the kids alone. As they were walking out of the door, Vincent and Zander walked up, bowed and walked into Aurica's room. Jet was happy that they were there now; Conrad was a good kid, but Jet still didn't want his two daughters alone with him. Vincent drew closer to Phykira's side, and Zander to Aurica's. When Conrad put Aurica down, and waited for Zander to reach them, Zander cautiously continued walking toward Aurica, who was watching and waiting to see what would happen.

Phykira was ready to have Vincent split them up if they started fighting, and sure enough, Conrad picked a fight with Zander as soon as they were face to face. Vincent quickly got in-between them by pushing both with an arm, and growling, "This is not how a Prince should act, and a guard certainly isn't allowed to fight with a Prince!"

Zander quickly apologized. Vincent was his superior, and if he decided that Zander wasn't fit to protect Aurica, the other guards and captains would trust his judgment. Conrad walked toward Vincent and said, "And you have no right to tell me what to do."

Vincent didn't argue. He walked back to where Phykira still stood, and simply said, "Forgive me. I know that I was out of place, but it's my duty to protect both princesses, and I will not have you two roughhousing in their presence."

Looking away, Conrad said, "Humph, whatever... Just don't let it happen again."

Calcifer entered in his human form before anyone could leave, and walked over to the boys, who were still glaring at each other. Vincent bowed to him, and seeing the action, Zander and Conrad looked over to see whom he was bowing to, tensing as they saw Calcifer approaching them. Calcifer stopped in front of all three of them and snarled, "If any of you *ever* fight in front of Aurica or Phykira again, you WILL regret it."

He then cut through them and walked over to Aurica, who was happy to see him. Conrad walked over to Aurica and Zander, offering his goodbye to Aurica, before turning to Zander and hissing, "Just wait until we spar!"

Without another word, the young prince turned sharply on his heel and walked out of the room.

Zander's back straightened in anger, but Phykira was just glad that the altercation was over. The two boys had just met recently; and already hated each other. She knew that Zander hated Conrad because the older boy was mean, and was constantly saying that Zander was worthless, but had no idea where Conrad's dislike of the young guard came from.

Vincent clapped his hands, and once everyone had turned to face him, said, "Well, now that fun time is over, Zander, we should go report to the captain."

A fearful glimmer entered Zander's eyes, but he nodded his affirmation. They both bowed and walked out of the room. After they shut the door, two guards moved into position at the door, standing outside of it. Phykira picked Aurica up once more, walking over to the girl's bed and tucking her beneath the blankets. Brushing a wisp of hair from Aurica's forehead, Phykira said, "You should go to bed, it's been a long day."

Aurica nodded sleepily, already nodding off. Phykira quietly slipped from the room and went to her own room to do the same.

~~~~~~

When Vincent opened the door to the captain's room, Zander briefly hesitated, but went in to take whatever punishment he deserved. Zander waited by the door while Vincent went up to the captain and gave him his report. After Vincent filled the captain in on the incident, they both gestured for Zander to come forward. The captain was older, with dark thinning hair and yellow eyes; he was a big man, with muscles that would make most men run. Even though he had the highest respect for the Queen, he refused to help the humans, and liked that Jet took care of it. He respected Jet very much, and supported him with almost whatever the king needed. He looked at Zander with stern eyes and voice as he said, "Vincent tells me you got into a fight with Prince Conrad. Now while he's a brat, and he deserves to be punched; he *is* a prince, and to make matters worse, you fought with him right in front of the princesses! Just like you, Aurica is young and impressionable; if she sees you fighting, she might start hitting people. And while Phykira is old enough to know that it's wrong, she still could've been hurt! Now, do you understand why this will not be tolerated again?"

Zander stood tall and in a strong voice, replied, "Yes sir! I take full responsibility for my actions, and I promise it'll never happen again."

The captain leaned back into his chair, and in the same stern voice said, "Very good. Though I doubt that this will never happen again, however, remember that you are never to engage him. I don't care if he punches you! You are never to fight with him, or anyone else, outside of the training facilities, is that clear?"

Zander straightened once more and loudly said, "Yes sir!"

Smiling at the young boy's eagerness, the captain announced that there was a new, young guard in the training hall at that moment, and that Zander should go meet him. Curious, they left the room; with Vincent patting Zander on the back and saying, "You'll make a fine guard, Zander! You took that very well."

Zander smiled as they returned to the training room.

The young guard was still in there, training, He was impressive with the sword, and he looked like he was good with other weapons as well. He stopped when they walked down to the training floor, snapping to attention when he saw the captain. "Good day, Captain. I'm Fenris Lunis, of Luminatos; world of the light dragons."

The captain had a stern look on his face, but he didn't want to smile the first time they met. "Well met, Fenris. This is Zander, a personal guard of Princess Aurica."

Fenris turned to Zander. "Nice to meet you, Zander."

After a quick discussion, Zander and Fenris followed the elders out of the training hall and listened intently as the captain gave them a better tour of the castle. The dragon-humanoids believed in starting training extremely early; Zander was only five, and Fenris was six, but they still got to enjoy their childhood when their day of training was over.

~~~~~~

Queen Akira was in her study. It had been a several months since she had revealed her condition to Jet, and she was expecting the baby any day now. Stealing a few moments for herself, once again she was writing in her diary.

"I have consulted with Ignis, and he has predicted that the baby is a boy! I've always wanted a son; I love my daughters, and I know they'll make great older sisters, but I want to give Jet a son. Aurica is getting so big. She just turned three, and is more active than ever. I'm a little worried that my boy might be the same way, as Phykira was never like this when she was younger. Jet has his hands full with the latest war that has begun on Ariliria, feeling that he needs to help his home world. Rayne adores him now; and takes him there whenever he wants, as she knows that I shouldn't be moving too much this close to birth.

"Phykira and her dragon Abyss are doing great. Their teamwork is so synchronized and beautiful to watch; and Aurica and Calcifer are an amazing team as well. The link between them; and their shared ability to read emotions and minds, is rather strange. Ignis confessed that neither he, nor his partner, had that power, nor has Phykira shown any signs of special powers. It could be because Aurica is a half-breed; the genes from her human father gifting her with powers we haven't seen before. If that's the case for her, I can't help but wonder what kind of powers, or type of dragon, my son will have. Ignis is saying that it's hard to tell, just like it was with Aurica, but he thinks it's going to be an Ice Dragon."

Hearing someone approach the door, Akira quickly put her diary away and rose unsteadily to her feet as she realized who it was.

The door opened and Jet stumbled in, covered in blood. He had barely cleared the door before he collapsed. Akira ran toward him as swiftly as her pregnant body allowed, yelling for the guards to send for the healers. Phykira; hearing the commotion, ran into see what was happening, only to find Jet lying on the floor. She dropped to her knees beside her mother as Akira picked his head up off the floor, placing it in her lap so that he wouldn't be lying completely on the stone. Akira immediately began to heal him, with Phykira joining in. While the princess hadn't yet learned a lot about healing, she knew enough to assist her mother.

The guards ran to Akira's side, pleading, "Please, Queen Akira, stop! It's not good for you to use this much energy in your condition, and the healers are on their way!"

Akira ignored them; continuing to pour her healing power into her husband, so that Jet was almost completely healed when the healers arrived. Akira suddenly stopped and just sat there; Phykira copying the older woman's actions as she turned to study her mom. A small cry escaped the princess as Akira fluttered her eyes and collapsed to the side in exhaustion. The healers, who had already begun working on Jet, glanced up at Phykira's cry, paling as they saw their unconscious queen. Several of them stopped working on Jet and turned their attention to Akira, fearful for their queen's life and that of her unborn child.

Phykira knew that she would only be in the way, and as she rose to her feet, she spotted Aurica walking into the study. Hurrying over to her in an attempt to block what the healers were doing, she grabbed Aurica by the arm as the half-asleep child mumbled, "Sissy, I want to see."

Phykira picked her up and murmured, "Mom is having the baby, and we would just be in the way, so let's go somewhere else."

Zander runs up to them, bows, and asks, "Princess Phykira, what's going on?"

Phykira replied, "I think my mom is giving birth, so Aurica and I are staying out of the way".

"Oh, is that so?" A voice from behind them inquires. They both turn around and see Lord Ernest and Prince Conrad emerging from the shadows of the hall. Ernest steps forward first and his son follows him, smirking at Zander. Ernest hadn't even noticed Zander, but when he did he harshly demanded, "What is this wretch doing here?!?"

Zander tried to look tough, answering, "I am training to be Princess Aurica's personal guard, my lord."

Ernest looked at him with disgust before turning away. Even though Conrad enjoyed picking on Zander, he still wondered why his father acted the way he did towards the younger boy. He thought that his father went overboard with his harshness, but would never say that to the older man. Zander just looked forward and stood his ground. Vincent appeared out of the shadows and started clapping. "Very well done, Zander."

Ernest looked at Zander again with newfound resentment. Zander noticed, but didn't look away from Vincent. Phykira asked Vincent what Ernest's problem was, to which the guard replied, "It's a secret, I'm afraid. Forgive me, my princess, but Zander and I must be going. Good day to you, Princess Phykira, Princess Aurica, Lord Ernest, Prince Conrad".

Watching as both guards left, Ernest looked at Phykira and said, "Why would they train that wretch to be Princess Aurica's guard? He's not worthy in the least!"

Phykira coldly stared at the man, her tone prim as she replied, "I don't know, Lord Ernest. I'm told that the guards only pick candidates that they think will make excellent guards. If I may ask, what do you have against Zander? He's a nice boy, and from what I have seen, this is the first time he's ever met you."

Ernest looked up, his eyes remote as he replied, "He is... I'm sorry, Princess Phykira, but that is something personal. I hope that you can understand, but I can't talk about it."

At his refusal, Conrad, Phykira and Aurica all looked down in disappointment. Turning to his son, Lord Ernest growled, "Let's go, Conrad."

Nodding at his father's command, Conrad quietly offered, "Until next time, Princess."

~~~~~~

Vincent and Zander were still walking, and Zander was still wondering what he did to make Lord Ernest so upset. He didn't think he had done anything wrong, but with Lord Ernest, there didn't need to be a reason. He slowed down, lost in his own thoughts, and when Vincent stopped, Zander didn't notice and almost walked into him, stopping just in time. Glancing down at his protégé with a smile, Vincent offered, "Don't' think about it too much".

Zander looked up, softly inquiring, "Permission to speak, sir?"

Vincent became serious, replying, "Permission granted, trainee."

Zander straightened up, meeting Vincent's eyes as he asked, "If I may ask, do you know what I did to make Lord Ernest so angry with me? You were standing there the whole time, so you must've seen what I did wrong".

Vincent couldn't help it, he cracked up laughing. Zander was confused by the reaction, but didn't waver. Vincent's laughter stopped and he said, "You did nothing wrong, he just doesn't like some people. On another note, I am very impressed. I wasn't hiding it well but, I was still testing you, and you passed. Even more, you didn't back down after Lord Ernest yelled at you, you remained at Phykira's and Aurica's side. You're going to be a guard in no time if you keep this up!"

~~~~~~

After Ernest and Conrad had finished talking with Princess Phykira and Princess Aurica, they started their journey home. Conrad kept pace with his father and said, "Father, though I don't like Zander either, but you seem to really hate him… Why?"

Ernest stopped abruptly, and said, "You'll understand when you're older, but right now it's no concern of yours."

Ernest began walking again and Conrad nodded and followed after him.

~~~~~~

Aurica snuck past Phykira; who was still wondering what Zander could have done to make Lord Ernest so angry, tiptoeing towards their mother's chamber. Deciding that they'd waited long enough, Phykira turned around to tell Aurica that they should go see if their mother was ok, only to find that Aurica was one step ahead of her. She quickly caught up to Aurica and said, "You didn't have to sneak away, Aurica. I'm worried about her too."

Aurica just smiled and started skipping. They entered the room to find the doctor holding a baby, and with squeals of excitement, they ran over to see if they had a baby brother or sister. The nurses see the princesses running towards the newborn, and attempt to stop them, saying, "You two should know better!"

One of the nurses extended her hands and gestured for them to hold her hands, and once they had done so, she led them over to see the baby and their mother. As they drew close enough to see, the doctor placed the baby in Akira's arms, and smiling when they reached her bedside, the queen softly exclaimed, "It's a boy! What should I name him?"

Jet had regained consciousness during the birth, and walked over to his daughters. They realized that Akira was talking to him, when he replied, "I have a good name for him. How about Rai..? No Raiko?"

Princess Phykira pushed in closer to her mother and baby brother, reaching out to hold his hand as she said, "Hello Raiko! I'm your big sister, Phykira."

Aurica scooted in closer, climbing onto the bed with them to coo and smile at her new brother. While they are all gathered around the queen's bed, Ignis contacted Akira, announcing, "It's as I thought! Your son has an Ice dragon. I'll open a portal for the hatchling now."

A portal suddenly opened right next to Raiko, and a small blue-gray dragon appeared. The dragon immediately crawled to Raiko, curling around the baby. Akira wondered if the dragon was able to speak yet, and softly asked the dragon what its name was. The dragon looked at her, blinked its eyes several times, and quietly replied that her name was Glacey.

Astonished that yet another dragon could speak at birth; they turn to Aurica and ask her if she could call Calcifer in. Calcifer was already there, hiding in the corner; and at the request, he walked up to them. Queen Akira asked him to turn back into his natural form, and with a shrug, he transformed back into a dragon. He looked down at Glacey, who in turn looked up at him. They had expected Glacey to have abnormal traits, but the only one that seemed strange, was she was slightly grayer than most ice dragons. Raiko didn't appear to have any abnormal traits to him either; other than his hair, which resembled Glacey's scales, and both of their eyes were a beautiful ice blue. Glacey couldn't read minds, however, but her mental link with Raiko was still very strong.

Ignis informed Akira that there weren't any complications with Glacey, and that he believed that he'd already made his choice, but would wait until the appropriate time to be absolutely sure. Akira allowed no emotion to show on her face, but she worried about how Phykira would react if Aurica or Raiko ascended instead. With that thought, she realized that Phykira might not be the right choice if she felt jealousy toward her younger siblings. As Akira was watching her children, Phykira glanced at her mother, smile at her, and then looked down at her new baby brother. Akira relaxed, thinking that it might not be an issue in this case. '...*I guess in eight years it'll all be settled...*"

Part 8

Rikku, the Electric Dragon

Elefon made another surprise visit to Azelia, but this time he brought a young girl with him. She had black hair and orange eyes, and despite her unusual characteristics, she was an electric dragon just like Elefon. She was wearing an orange tunic, with a black belt wrapped around her waist, black leggings, and orange shoes. Elefon looked anxious as he walked with her, and reacting to his emotions, she had her arms crossed defensively over her chest, with her head held high. They were walking through the hall when they caught Aurica's attention, and within seconds, she was peering around the corner at them, trying to figure out who the intruders were. She wasn't used to seeing Elefon anymore and especially not with someone else in tow. Elefon noticed her and speed walked over to her, while the girl kept her pace, and didn't make eye contact with Aurica. Peering down at the young girl, he softly questioned, "Princess Aurica, what are you doing?"

Aurica ducked back behind the pillar and then peered back over, replying, "Nothing, I was just going to find Vincent, have you seen him?"

He shook his head while Aurica looked over at the girl and then back at Elefon. He looked back at his companion before suddenly clapping his hands, startling both girls and forcing them to look up at him. "Right! Princess Aurica, this young girl with me is Rikku, and I'm going to ask your parents to take her into the castle for a while. Are they in the throne room?"

Rikku looked away, while Aurica simply nodded and pointed in the direction of the throne room, before gesturing that they should follow her. They started walking there together, with Aurica skipping along next to

Elefon, while looking back at Rikku periodically. When they were almost there, Aurica looked at Rikku again, and in response the dragon stuck out her tongue. Aurica quickly looked away, and Rikku went back to ignoring her surroundings. Aurica didn't look back again after that, and Elefon chuckled as he walked slowly to accommodate the short strides of both little girls.

Their journey to the throne room passed in silence until they arrived and the guards opened the doors. Only Jet was in attendance, and Aurica ran over to him, while Elefon and Rikku kept their pace. Rikku was falling behind as she looked around, but caught up to Elefon easily. Smiling at the sight of their visitors, Jet held out his hand in the Ariliria custom, declaring, "Lord Elefon, it's so nice to see you again! What brings you here, and who's the girl?"

Nodding at the warm welcome he'd been given, Elefon returned, "Jet, it is nice to see you again as well. The girl is Rikku, and she's the reason I'm here. I would like to request that she stay here for a while."

Jet looked at Rikku, and she looked back at him, and then at Aurica. "Do I *have* to stay here Elefon?"

Elefon looked down at her. "Yes, but not for very long, so don't worry."

Rikku turned around and ran out of the room, with Aurica following quickly after her. Jet and Elefon each reached out an arm to stop her, but she was already almost to the door. They turned back to each other, and with a shrug, Jet stated, "I don't see why not. It looks like Aurica has already taken a shine to her; I've never seen her run after someone like that before."

Elefon nodded, sighed, and then bowed. "Thank you, Lord Jeticous. I'll be on my way then."

"Thank you for dropping by, Lord Elefon." Grimacing as a crash sounded from somewhere in the castle, Jet added, "We'll take good care of Rikku."

Aurica had gone after Rikku, but had yet to find her. It had been quite a while since the other girl had stormed out, but there had been no sign of her since she'd left the throne room. Mumbling to herself as she was walking, she passed Vincent and some guards, sighing as Vincent questioned, "Princess Aurica, where are you off to?"

Aurica didn't bother to stop, but turned around and started walking backwards, replying, "I'm looking for Rikku, bye now."

She turned back around to walk normally again, leaving Vincent and the others to look at each other with puzzled expressions.

"Who's Rikku? Do you know Vincent?" He shook his head, and they continued walking, wondering what game the little princess was playing this time.

Rikku was walking around aimlessly, following corridor after corridor, until she finally spotted someone she recognized. Marching up to the princess, she asked, "Aurica right? Has Lord Elefon left yet? Show me back to the throne room now!"

Quirking an eyebrow as she'd seen her sister do, Aurica replied, "Yes, I'm Aurica, and yes, he has. Just continue down this hall and you'll find it soon enough... And for future reference, I'm a princess, and you can't order me around."

Rikku half smirked before she left in the direction Aurica had indicated. Aurica stood there for a couple minutes, pondering, "Wait, wasn't I looking for someone before this?"

Rikku found Jet, and after confirming that Elefon had left, he showed her around the castle, trying to explain routes through it so that she wouldn't get lost. After several minutes of walking quietly, she softly asked, "Why do I have to be here? Did he say anything?"

Jet stopped and looked at her. "He didn't say why, but sometimes we'll exchange children with each other, in order to teach them the ways of other planets. However, I don't think we did a transfer for you, but as it just happened today, I'm sure we'll be sending someone over there."

The next day Aurica was out on the balcony when Rikku peeked around the column at her. "Aurica? Can we talk?"

Aurica nodded and led the other girl to a side balcony. "What did you want to talk about, Rikku?"

Rikku turned toward the outside, her face closed off, as she said, "It's nothing really... I just want to call a truce with you, for the time that I'm here."

Aurica smiled and went up to the railing too. "Sure, a truce sounds good to me."

They spent some time making up a secret handshake, which didn't take them long, and when they were done, Phykira came around the corner and saw them. Quirking an eyebrow, she inquired, "Do I even want to know what you two are up too?"

They smiled at her, looked at each other, and then charged at her; splitting up and running down different halls. She signed, and murmured to herself, "I knew it; I *don't* want to know."

~~~

The days that followed Rikku's arrival were crazy and fun, for her and Aurica, at least; Vincent had to clean up after them. Phykira helped him a few times, but he would stop her, saying it wasn't work for a princess. That irritated Phykira, and she would counter with the fact that Aurica had been involved, and she *was* her responsibility. She liked spending time with him, even if it was because Aurica and Rikku were mischievous. Most of the time she'd stop helping and just talk to him, which he liked.

During one such moment he glanced at her, posing, "Phykira, I was wondering about something."

She rose from where she'd been working and went over to him, asking, "What were you wondering about?"

He stopped what he was doing, turning to face her fully as he began, "It's about the future..."

Rikku ran in at that moment and went directly to Phykira. "Phykira, I can't find Aurica; have you seen her?"

Phykira shook her head and looked at Vincent, to find that he was looking at her as well.

Phykira's gaze met Vincent's, and with a nod, she grabbed his hand, following Rikku to find Aurica. Vincent was good at finding the princess, and sure enough, he found her sneaking around in the vents. "Princess, what are you doing? You're going to get hurt."

She shook her head, but climbed out anyway. "I was fine Vincent; you worry too much."

'You have no idea...' He warily thought to himself. Phykira came down the hallway, and when she saw all the soot and dust on the floor, she stopped and looked at Aurica. As she opened her mouth to chastise the younger girl, Rikku came running through, and smacked Aurica on the back, yelling, "You're it!!!"

As Rikku took off once more, Aurica gave Vincent a glare, and took off after Rikku. Clenching his fists, he snarled. "She made me find Aurica for this!? They're both driving me insane!"

Phykira was just as angry at the family's ward, but tamped down her emotions. Realizing that she was staring at Vincent after his outburst, she blushed furiously as their eyes met, and they both looked down.

A few days later; Jet was walking through the castle with an unconscious Aurica in his arms. She had hurt her ankle, and in an effort to heal herself, she had used up all of her energy and fainted. Vincent suddenly ran up to him, exclaiming, "King Jet! There is a problem, sire! The captain requests that you please report to the audience chamber… Oh, you have Aurica! I can take her."

Jet nodded, and handed Aurica to Vincent. "She's hurt her ankle, so please take care of her. Thanks Vincent."

Vincent kept walking in the direction of Aurica's room, and she woke up, confused to find herself in the guard's arms. Frowning, she questioned, "Vincent? Why are you carrying me? Where's my dad?"

Vincent looked down at her with a smile. "He had some business to attend to, so he asked me to return you to your room. I heard that you hurt your ankle; what were you thinking trying to use healing magic? You're a fire dragon, Princess; even a small bit of healing magic is dangerous."

She started tearing up at his words and pressed her head into his chest. Vincent felt bad, but it was better that she became angry at him, rather than her father.

They reached her room, and when he sat her down on the bed, she rolled over and curled into a ball. Vincent scratched his head, closed his eyes, and walked away. *'Man, she's a handful! Phykira was never like this, and hopefully Raiko doesn't start acting like her either. This guard job is a lot more troublesome than I thought it'd be, but in a few years, it'll all be over.'*

He almost ran into Akira as he exited Aurica's room, and offering a short bow, he informed her, "Queen Akira, I'm sorry to be the bearer of bad news, but it appears that Aurica has injured her ankle."

Akira nodded and turned into Aurica's room, intent on healing her child's ankle as she said, "Thank you, Vincent. I heard the captain say that he was looking for you."

He nodded, bowed once more, and then left. As the guard's footsteps faded, Akira sat on Aurica's bed, frowning as she saw the damage to the joint. Aurica had rolled back over when she heard her mother's voice, and she winced at the pain that lashed through her at the motion. Akira gently took Aurica's foot in her hand, shaking her head as she questioned, "How did you manage this? I can see that you tried to heal yourself, Aurica, and there is a reason that it didn't work. Your strength doesn't lie in healing magic; you should know this by now. You may have some ability for magic, but you need to stop trying to use it in that way. One of these days you're going to go too far, and neither the healers, nor I, may be able to help you."

As Akira spoke, a blue light enveloped Aurica's ankle and Akira's hands, sending healing warmth to repair the damage, and with the strength of Akira's power, it didn't take long to heal. Akira was cautiously flexing the ankle when Phykira walked in, with Raiko following behind her. "Hey, mom; hey, Aurica. Mom, Raiko wanted to see you."

Raiko was three now, and he still showed no signs of being as energetic as Aurica, and they were all relieved about that. He ran ahead and tripped; and picking him up, Phykira admonished, "Raiko, you shouldn't run!"

She put him down, where he patted himself off with a frown, and then ran to his mother. Phykira put her hand on her head, thinking, 'He's like Aurica, in the way he refuses to listen to me!'

Enjoying the moment of family togetherness, they all sat on Aurica's bed, with Raiko on Akira's lap, while Phykira and Aurica were playing around with a silly game they'd made up. Jet and Vincent walked in soon after to find them all still ensconced on Aurica's bed, playing a guessing game. Phykira saw Vincent, and jumped up to greet him and her father. Aurica began playing with Raiko as Akira rose gracefully to her feet to greet Jet. Jet had a few new scrapes, and Vincent had a couple too. "What were you two doing? Hold on I'll heal you both."

Akira started on Jet at Vincent's request, and while Phykira wanted to try to heal Vincent, he stopped her. "You aren't suited for healing magic either, Princess… Besides, they're just scratches, so don't worry about me, my princess."

'Not suited?' Depression and a sense of failure pressed on her at his words, confusing Vincent until he realized that she had taken his words the wrong way. Reaching out a hand to stop her as she stormed towards the door, he called, "Phykira wait, I didn't mean it in a bad way."

Phykira paused slightly at his words, turning to meet his gaze with devastated eyes, before she nodded and ran out of the room.

'Oh great, I have to work on thinking about what I say to her more and more lately.' He left the room to go find her; Akira and Jet watching him go with speculation shining in their eyes, while Aurica and Raiko hadn't noticed a thing.

Phykira had run off to a mid-sized balcony, not far from the royal family's chambers. It was the place that she went to whenever she was upset, and one that Vincent had made note of years ago. Vincent easily found her and slowly walked up to her, softly stating, "You know that wasn't the way I meant it."

She turned around. "Yeah I know; I came out here for a different reason."

He walked to the balcony railing and put his hands on it. "What was the reason then?"

Phykira remained where she was, not facing him as she replied, "It's nothing, maybe some other time."

"Phykira, I..." Allowing his words to trail off as her back stiffened, Vincent offered her a bow, murmuring, "As you wish, Princess."

Stalking from the balcony and down the hall, he paused to glance back at the young woman on the balcony, knowing that one day, things would be quite different.

Ever since Rikku had come to live at the castle, she and Aurica got into much more trouble than they each would have found on their own. They participated in play fighting more than anything, frustrating the household with their antics each day. Rikku wasn't afraid to be herself, and Aurica not only admired that about her, but had begun to adopt the mindset herself. They caused Vincent and the other guards more than their fair share of trouble, and though Aurica felt bad about her behavior at first, she discovered that she was having too much fun to stop. She had always had Conrad, Vincent and Zander around; as well as her sister, but Phykira was ten years older, so it was easier for her to relate to Rikku.

Pushing his thoughts of the young princess and her companion from his mind, Vincent went to his room, reluctant to go any further in his conversation with Phykira. He loved her; and she loved him, he knew that, but their positions threatened the relationship building between them. He

lay back on his bed, thinking of his past; and of his father, who had told him
the story every time he asked.

~~~~~~

*...70 years ago, the war between the Simiera dragons and the "rebels", led
by Kaisa, ended abruptly. The world the time dragons had begun calling home
was destroyed, but worse yet, was the death of a person. While many died; each
important in their own way, the death of this one person sent the king of Azelia
into a rage. In the space of mere seconds he went berserk; going from a typical
fire dragon-humanoid, into a blue fire dragon, because the one killed was his
daughter, princess Azelia, for whom the planet was named...*

This is the story that was passed down by Vincent's father, the older
man having lived through it all. The time dragons lived the longest, aging
very slowly, but because of this, however, they are dependent longer in their
youth. Vincent always wondered why Cerek, the time world, was destroyed,
but Azelia wasn't. His father had always said that it was because Cerek was
closer and more involved in the war, and as Kaisa's brother, Raizen, was a
time dragon, it was likely punishment that both planets would be destroyed.
Azelia had just barely managed to hold on, but Kaisa's rage made it more
unstable, and the Simiera dragons deemed that fair; after all, they didn't
think the planet would last much longer.

Even with the justification made by his father, Vincent began to loath
the fire dragons and the current line of royalty. When his father, Zen, died
before Vincent turned 10, he decided to infiltrate the castle, and slowly
seek his revenge. But first, he'd have to get to Azelia. He'd never had a time
dragon come to him; making him weaker, and he couldn't reform the planet
by himself. Just like the fire dragons, time dragons were extremely rare, so he
knew he'd have to use the Queen, or one of her descendants, to accomplish
the mission he'd set for himself. He was currently on Nieve, the ice planet,
and though the ice dragons had been kind enough to take in refugees, they
warned them that life would be tough. Vincent's father had never had any
problems, in fact, he had thrived in the subzero temperatures.

One day in the trade market, which never saw very much traffic, Vincent
noticed a very young couple, who were not much older than he was. He didn't
know why, but he was drawn to them. The boy had yellow hair and eyes, and
the girl had silver hair and green eyes. They were talking, when he went over

to them and gave the girl a hug. She looked like a time dragon, but, she was a wind dragon. She got that reaction a lot, though not usually in the form of a hug. The three of them instantly bonded. The boy was named Micah, and the girl was Aria, and they were on their way to Azelia. When they offered to take Vincent with them, he accepted without a second thought.

They weren't going to stay long, but Vincent intended on staying longer, so they helped him find a place to live. After they left, Vincent thought of multiple ways to get into the castle, but he couldn't think of one where he didn't get killed. He knew that the royal couple had a child, so they were going to be very protective and not take chances with her safety. One day he went up a hill to a lone sapling and practiced with a sword until he saw shadows moving above him. Glancing up as panic filled him; he discovered that it was the royal guard. The captain brought himself to the ground by controlling the dirt, levitating it and using it to transport himself and the other members of the guard. He looked at Vincent with a puzzled expression. Running his hand through his thick brown hair, his deep brown eyes showed concern and acceptance as studied the young child with blistered hands. His voice was surprisingly caring as he asked, "What are you doing here, young one?"

"Just practicing sir!" he blurted out. Panic showed on his face; his yellow eyes dilating and his breaths shortening as he watched the captain move closer. The captain took a moment; realizing he was standing over a frightened child, and backed off with a chuckle.

"Oh my! Forgive me son, I didn't mean to frighten you." He let out a laugh that came from the very bottom of his stomach; tears almost forming as he continued to belly laugh.

"Oh, no, I wasn't scared, just… umm… Surprised, is all. Did I do something wrong?" he said with his head held high.

Continuing to chuckle, the captain boomed, "Is that so? Interesting! You know what kid? I like you, you're a tough one. Come with me!"

Without warning, the ground under the captain began lifting into the air, the dirt making a loose staircase that led up to him. Vincent hesitated, but only for a moment. This was it, this was his chance! He knew what to do; he'd become a guard! That is when he saw the black-haired princess playing in the courtyard below, with a yellow haired boy as her companion. Excitement filled him as he realized that he was one step closer to completing his mission; a mission he could not fail.

Part 9

The First Signs of Trouble

'The deadline to the time of truth is drawing near. Phykira is sixteen, Aurica is six; almost seven, and Raiko is four. Only four more years...' Akira thought to herself, before murmuring, "Well, only time will tell".

"Who are you talking to, my Queen?" A solider had entered and was stunned to find that the queen was alone and appeared to be talking to an empty room.

Flushing in irritation at having been caught talking to herself, she waved her hand dismissively, stating, "I was just thinking out loud. Do you have something to report?"

The soldier straightened, replying, "Yes your highness! I have a report from Vincent that Aurica is missing, and that Zander has gone to look for her. The other soldiers have already left to assist in the search!"

A slight look of concern crossed Akira's face, before she then smiled. The soldier didn't move or say anything, but became concerned at the queen's lack fear for her daughter's safety. Shaking her head at his expression, Akira said, "Don't worry so much, Calvin. Aurica is fine; she has a habit of wandering off, but I can sense that she's with Calcifer, so there is nothing to worry about. Zander and Conrad are moving closer to her location as we speak."

Calvin bowed in relief, and then turned to leave and notify the captain that Princess Aurica was safe.

~*~*~

On her way to the dragons nest, Aurica went through the main gate, but the guards noticed her immediately, and went up to her, inquiring, "Princess Aurica, what are you doing out here?"

Aurica looked up at them, flashing them a bright smile as she replied, "Calcifer and I are going to the dragons' nest, as I want to see the townspeople's dragons."

He nodded and signaled the guards in the towers to raise the gate. After the gate was open, he said, "Princess? We shall not get in your way, but if you could wait for some guards to arrive to accompany you, we would feel better about opening this gate."

Aurica was a sweet girl, so she didn't just blow off their concern. "That won't be necessary. Calcifer is with me, and he is more than capable of protecting me."

Smiling, she gave them a little wave as she stepped through the gate and into the town. Many of the townsfolk noticed her entering, all bowing low in respect, and elbowing the ones that hadn't noticed the princesses' arrival. Turning at the assault on their bodies to meet the others' gaze, the rest of the villagers discovered their visitor and quickly bowed as well. As Aurica simply waved at them, she noticed that one of the people had dropped something, so she walked up to them, picked the item up, and handed it to the owner. Flushing at the attention, the item's owner bowed deeply as she accepted her belonging. Aurica continued walking toward her destination, while Calcifer followed behind her, ignoring all of the looks they were receiving.

Many of the town's people looked around for guards that should be somewhere close by in order to protect the princess, but all they saw were the two who were trailing far behind her and Calcifer. Aurica tripped as she neared the exit, causing a townsman to look around before he cautiously moved to help her; extending his hand to aid her. Aurica took the proffered hand, rising to her feet before thanking him. The guards trailing her finally noticed that she had fallen, and seeing the man so close to her, hurried over. The man made sure that she was okay before returning to his own business, and with a smile and another wave, Aurica and Calcifer left the town. As the guards passed the man, he straightened his back, hoping he wasn't going to be punished for touching the princess. They passed by him with a glance; their eyes telling him that this was the only time he'd get away with it. His wife ran to him with a sob, relieved that he hadn't been punished for his kind action, never knowing that if the guards had tried to punish the man, Aurica wouldn't have allowed it.

The way to the dragons nest wasn't a very long journey, but it was a good distance away. On the way Aurica encountered Conrad and Zander, who were as far away from each other as they could be. They started walking with her as she passed by them, smiling at the way they threw each other hate-filled glowers. Glancing over her shoulder, she announced, "I'm going to visit the dragon nests!"

Sighing at her words, Conrad exchanged a silent look with Calcifer, seeing his own concern for the princesses' safety mirrored in the dragon's eyes. Closing ranks around her, Conrad softly questioned, "Aurica, do your parents know where you are?"

Sighing at his inquiry, Aurica, replied, "Of course not, or I wouldn't be here. But I need to see the dragons, Conrad. I may be responsible for them one day, so I should get to know them, don't you think?"

Sighing again in resignation, Conrad shook his head and continued to follow the princess to the gate of the dragon nest. Entering behind her, he watched as her eyes filled with awe at the great number of dragons that filled the nest.

"Look at them all!!" Aurica pointed at the dragons that had come to see her and her companions. Conrad moved closer to her in order to look at the dragons as well, feeling extremely protective of her. He would die to save her, and Zander was the same way; their only concern was to protect her from anything that could possibly hurt her. Calcifer almost left because he knew Aurica would be more than safe with them; they were getting along at the moment, and when it came to Aurica, their teamwork was impeccable, but Aurica wanted him there, so there he remained. Though it had originally just been the two of them that set out to see the dragons nest, the other two had come searching for Aurica, so her adventure had obviously been noted by the palace. Not wanting the queen to worry, he was sure to send Akira news of what was going on.

An ice dragon suddenly flew over toward them, calling, "Welcome, Princess Aurica!"

Aurica smiled brightly. "Hello, Mr. Ice Dragon."

He landed close to them, much to Calcifer's dismay, and when the ice dragon noticed Calcifer's discomfort, he said, "Your dragon is still much too small for you to ride on to achieve the full experience, so how would you like to ride on my back?"

Aurica looked back at Calcifer, noting that he wasn't pleased with the idea, but accepting of the fact that the ice dragon was right. Knowing that he was okay with it, she approached the ice dragon and he made it easier for her to get on his back by drifting off of the cliff. Aurica jumped down onto his back, and as they took off, Calcifer transformed into a dragon and joined their flight. It was much different on the ice dragons' back. It was so cold that her teeth chattered, even though he was trying to make it more comfortable for her. The view was incredible, and as many of the other dragons noticed the princess on the ice dragon, they joined them in the air; not only for fun, but to protect her as well. Most everyone who came into Aurica's presence was driven by the need to protect her.

They were up there for several minutes when Aurica noticed some people nearby; and as they looked like they were waiting for something, Aurica didn't think about it too much. The wind on her face, and the fact that all of the other dragons were up there with her, made her happy. She looked down at the boys and wondered why they weren't up there with her. With almost all of the dragons in the sky with her, she felt so happy, as though she were meant to fly with them.

"AURICA!!"

She wildly looked around for several seconds before realizing that it was Ignis that had just contacted her. All of the dragons were still in the air, but they were now hovering in one place around her. She closed her eyes and tried to contact him, replying, "Great fire dragon?"

She waited for a while, beginning to fear that her attempt at communication had failed, when his voice suddenly filled her mind once more. "Aurica, come see me immediately."

The ice dragon flew her to the cliff that she had come from, with Calcifer following. The dragons that were in the air were either clearing a path for the ice dragon, Aurica and Calcifer, or they were already back down on the ground. Conrad and Zander were looking at them with confused expressions, and jumping off of the dragons' back, Aurica turned around to thank him, before turning back to the boys, stating, "Ignis has summoned me."

They nodded, and all of them turned to leave.

The boys could accompany Aurica most of the way to Ignis' lair, but at a certain point they weren't allowed to pass. Both had a feeling they should ignore that rule just this once, but they followed the rules that had been trained into them and let her go by herself, although reluctantly. After the boys stopped following her, Aurica felt uneasy, even though Calcifer was with her. It wasn't just her; Calcifer was uneasy and thinking about turning around to get Conrad and Zander; but it was too late. A group of ten masked men suddenly appeared, attacking them from all directions.

The space was too small for Calcifer to transform into a dragon, so he powered up and started to attack, as did Aurica. The fight didn't last long, as the men easily overpowered them, knocking Aurica out and restraining Calcifer, which was no easy feat. It took seven of the attackers to subdue him, and even they had a tough time. One of the men was holding Aurica in his arms, while another took out what appeared to be a syringe. As he prepared to give Aurica the injection, the last man kept his eyes on Calcifer, alert for any signs of interference. The man giving the shot had half of it injected into Aurica by the time Vincent showed up, quickly taking out the man giving the shot and then the one holding Aurica. Unfortunately, the entire contents of the syringe had been administered, but now Vincent had her in his arms. Even when he was holding Aurica, he was taking out the assailants, and was joined by Conrad and Zander, who disabled the rest.

Vincent glared at the boys and took off to the castle, with Aurica crying out in pain. At the sound of her cries, Vincent increased his speed and flew in through the balcony window closest to the doctor's room. They were ready for her, but were not sure what the injection had been, as the syringe had been crushed in the fight. Vincent carefully set Aurica down on the table as Akira and Jeticous rushed in, and hurried to Aurica's side. Vincent bowed and left to find Conrad and Zander.

The doctors quickly discovered what the shot had been; a serum that was given to dragon-humanoids that were losing their dragon abilities, either due to old age, illness or severe injury.

"Why would they give this serum to her?" One of the doctors murmured, turning to the worried parents to announce, "The shot is slowly destroying what little human DNA she received from her father."

No one had noticed that Vincent was in the corner watching. He had found and scolded the boys for not noticing the danger sooner; ordering extra training as a punishment, before slipping back into the room where Aurica was being treated. Realizing that they were preparing to move the princess, he stepped into the shadows, making himself invisible in the confusion that still filled the room.

They all left the doctors room; with Jeticous carrying Aurica to her room, to find that Phykira was outside her sister's door, impatiently waiting for them. "Jet! What's wrong with Aurica?"

Jet looked at his stepdaughter with remorse filling his eyes. Whoever those men were, they were trying to destroy the minute human part of his daughter that she had received from him; a part so small as to be nearly insignificant, so was it truly that terrible? Forcing a smile onto his face, he replied, "Aurica is going to be okay. The attackers gave her an injection designed to destroy the human DNA she carries."

Phykira was in shock, and she was angry; her sister was perfect the way she was! And obviously it wasn't a bad thing that she had human in her; she had the rare fire dragon. Jeticous saw that she was just as angry as he was, but they let it go for the moment as they put Aurica in her bed and left the room. Phykira, Jet and Akira went to the audience chamber to discuss what had happened and a way to reverse the effects of the shot.

Inside Aurica's room Vincent was standing by her bed, studying the now-sleeping princess. "Will you be the one, Princess; the one to bring time back into existence?"

With a heavy sigh, he vanished.

~~~~~~~

They decided that the best course of action would be for Aurica to go to Ariliria for a little while. Phykira already had plans to go there to visit a friend she had met there before, so taking Aurica with her seemed like a natural solution. Once Aurica woke up she seemed fine, but they became concerned when they noticed that her eyes were darker than normal. She was told that she'd be going to Ariliria with her sister, but wasn't told what had happened. She had no objections, as she had always wanted to visit her father's home world. Raiko wanted to go too, but he was told he had to stay on Azelia. Even Aurica going there with Phykira was risky, but they felt they had no other choice; Aurica had to be on Ariliria, surrounded by humans, or she might become a blue fire dragon.

The day after Aurica woke up and was informed about what happened, and what she would have to do to reverse the affects, she and Phykira went to Ariliria. Phykira and Aurica rode on Abyss, and Calcifer flew alongside of them. It wasn't difficult to reach Ariliria, and even if Aurica had ridden on Calcifer he would have been fine, but they weren't sure how he'd react to Ariliria's atmosphere, so they decided not to take any chances.

Riding through the atmosphere was much harder than Calcifer had imagined. He was burning up himself and was happy that Aurica wasn't on him. *"I'll have to learn to control myself, as I can tell Aurica is going to want to come here again."* She looked back at him and nodded. Smiling, he flew closer and Aurica hopped onto him. Phykira led them down to where they could, and should, land in the future; it was a huge clearing that was close to a village, but this point was special. The dragons had used their powers to create an illusion so that anyone coming from their worlds would be concealed until the individuals touched the ground.

When they landed safely and dismounted the dragons, Calcifer transformed into his human form and Abyss took off. Phykira turned to face Aurica and Calcifer. "Now that we're here, you have to listen to what I say. I'm going to be meeting up with my friend, and Calcifer you should leave just as Abyss did. The fewer dragons around Aurica right now, the better."

Calcifer nodded, transformed and left. After he was gone Aurica followed Phykira through the forest until the sounds of a village could be heard in the distance. On the outskirts of the village there was a manor, and they turned there to where a man and his younger brother were waiting. The man started walking towards them with his brother trailing him. "Hello there Phykira, is this your sister?"

When Phykira smiled and nodded, the man knelt and introduced himself. "My name is Zeke, and the boy next to me is my younger brother, Levi."

Levi peaked around his brother's leg. "Hello, I'm Levi, nice to meet you."

Aurica looked up at her sister and then back at Zeke and Levi, "My name is Aurica, nice to meet you both."

With all of the introductions out of the way, Phykira and Zeke were getting ready to depart, when Phykira looked at the kids, saying, "We won't be gone long, so you two go play and get to know each other."

Zeke put his hand on Levi's head, ruffling the boy's hair as he ordered, "Be a man and show this young lady around."

Aurica and Levi were not too thrilled, but after their siblings left they turned to each other in resignation. Levi frowned, saying, "Aurica, Right? Well I guess I could show you around, but there isn't much to see though."

Aurica nodded and followed him.

As they were walking they saw some other children playing, but neither of them seemed to want to join them so they continued. *'My father's people sure are different from mom's people… Not in appearance, but in how they act, and dress. Sis must have made me wear these clothes to fit in more, and here I thought she was just playing dress up with me.'*

"Ummm… so how old are you Aurica?"

Aurica snapped out of her daydream and glanced at him. "I'm six, almost seven, how old are you, Levi?"

Realizing they're closer in age than he had thought, he smiled, replying, "I'm seven. I'm still a novice ninja, but in a couple years I'll be going on more missions."

Curious, Aurica stopped, forcing Levi to stop too. "What kinds of missions?"

He smirked, lifting his head up proudly as he replied, "I'll be going on missions to defend people and their cargo, or on infiltration missions, or for cooperation missions."

Smiling in interest and amusement, she started walking ahead of him, but he easily caught up and they ended up at a beautiful lake, one that Levi seemed both happy and disappointed to see. Even though he seemed to want to avoid the lake, he took her down to where there was a small dock, explaining, "This is where my brother and I train, but mainly Zeke."

They went to the edge of the dock, where there were some burn marks at the end and some on the corners. They were clearly using some type of fire. Levi started making signs with his hands and then he breathed out a fireball. He turned to Aurica, who was shocked and amazed. Since when did humans have power? He could tell she was thinking something along those lines, so he explained, "It's something only we ninjas who are trained in the fire discipline can do. Like I said, I'm still a novice, so my skills aren't that good yet."

Aurica studied him, thinking, 'He doesn't give himself enough credit... I want to give it a try.'

She turned back toward the water and executed her own fireball, but had to remain in control so that her dragon characteristics did not come out. The fireball was not as big as she could have made it, but any more power and she could have incinerated Levi and her dragon characteristic would overtake her human side.

Levi was not too surprised; his brother had mentioned that Aurica and her sister had unusual powers, and were fast learners. "Would you like to go to the next place?"

Turning back to him, she nodded with a smile.

On their way to the next place, Phykira and Zeke joined up with them, and immediately Phykira could tell that the effects of the shot were reversing, helped by the fact that Aurica now knew what she had to do to suppress it.

The next place was a training spot in a forest nearby. There, Levi asked Zeke to show all of them what he could do. Zeke had some knives on him, so he did as his brother asked. Zeke's moves were good; he was able to hit all of the targets, and for one of the moves he had to hit one knife with another. After his display, Phykira went to Aurica, softly saying, "It's time to leave Aurica. I think everything should be fine now."

Overhearing Phykira's words, Zeke and Levi looked over at them. Levi's face showed that he was sad about their departure, as they had grown close, even though it was only a short amount of time. Aurica felt the same way, but she was not feeling very well. It seemed it did not take long for her human side to take back over what had originally belonged to it, but now it was trying to take over more of her. They returned to the spot in the forest where Abyss and Calcifer were waiting.

~~~~~~

Once they returned to Azelia, the doctors were waiting to look at Aurica, and even though she was tired, she went with them in hopes that everything would be okay. She didn't want to lose the part of her that she received from her father; even if it did make her different.

The doctors seemed relieved when they came in with the test results; the human part of her was no longer in danger of being consumed by her dragon. "I must say, human DNA is very resilient and versatile."

Jet looked down at Aurica. "You didn't have to get the human part back. Life would be easier…."

Aurica looked up at him, so angry her small body was nearly shaking with it. "No dad! It's part of who I am, and I'm happy with who and what I am."

He smiled and hugged her for few minutes, secretly sobbing over her words as she patted him on the head. As Aurica was getting ready to go there was a knock at the door. Jet picked Aurica up and prepared to shield her from any attack while the nurse went to the door to open it. Tensing as the heavy portal opened, Jet relaxed as the door opened wide enough to reveal that Vincent was there with Phykira. Jet slowly put Aurica down, pondering, 'Why did I have such a strange feeling of danger?'

Phykira ran to Aurica to see what the doctors said, and Vincent was halfway there but then just stopped. Another nurse went up to Phykira, Aurica and Jet. "Princess Phykira, its good news! The effects of the injection were reversed and Princess Aurica is going to be just fine."

Phykira was relieved, and with a smile, said, "Aurica, Zander is waiting for you outside, you should go see him."

Aurica nodded with a smile and left to go see Zander.

Zander was pacing outside the doorway, and Conrad and Rikku were now there as well. Aurica smiled, and the boys both turned to her with frowns. She went to them and tried to think of a way to cheer them up, suggesting, "Let's go outside and play."

They just stared at her. "Aren't you mad at us?" Conrad asked, as Zander seemed to have the exact same question.

Ashamed of her own behavior, Aurica looked down, answering, "No, the whole thing was my fault. I told you I'd be fine with Calcifer; even though he was looking nervous too, and I ignored it."

Sometimes it seemed like Conrad and Zander could tell what the other was thinking. In unison, they both approached Aurica, got on one knee, and said together, "No my Princess, it was our fault. We know our duty and we should never have left you."

Rikku saw her opportunity and hit them both on the head. Aurica wanted to laugh, but she kept it to herself, but Rikku was a different story. The electric dragon was on the ground, laughing so hard she was crying.

~~~~~~~

A few days later Aurica was on the side balcony of the castle, upset about what had happened to her. As she sat contemplating the attack, she suddenly thought about what happened in a different way. If that stuff worked even a little; if it pushed away her human DNA long enough for her dragon side to become more dominant, then maybe her wings would finally come out… It was worth a try.

Rising to her feet, she carefully climbed onto the railing and jumped off. She could feel Calcifer nearby, rushing to her as he growled, "What were you thinking Aurica?"

She was able to get her wings out, but they were still too young; too immature, and failed her. She continued falling toward the chasm below, her screams swept away by the wind, when Zander flew in and caught her, with Calcifer arriving soon after. Calcifer transformed into his human form and poked her head, demanding, "What in the world were you thinking? Why would you jump off the balcony?"

When she didn't answer him, Calcifer growled in frustration and nodded for her to start walking. Within minutes Calcifer lead her into her mother's room and told Akira what had happened.

Her mother scolded her and then her father soon after. Zander was ordered to stay by her side at all times, until she promised never to do it again. She made several more attempts when Zander was called away; her last attempt almost killing her. Her wings came out and worked for a short while; just long enough for her to get high above the castle, but then the fragile extensions failed her, and she started to fall.

This time Vincent caught her and flew her back to the balcony she had jumped off of. "Princess, you must stop this; you could've gotten hurt or worse. Do you understand the danger you put yourself in, Aurica?"

She was looking down; crying, and forced Vincent to kneel down as he questioned, "Princess, what's wrong? I wasn't trying to yell at you, I just don't want to see you get hurt."

She leapt into him and he held her against his chest, murmuring, "It's ok, Aurica."

She was shaking her head into his chest. "No Vincent! W-why won't my wings work for me? What am I d-doing wrong?"

"You haven't done anything wrong." Vincent picked her up and carried her to her room, passing a few guards, who all asked what was wrong. Vincent gave all of them the same answer, "She's just upset, so I'm taking her to her room."

Vincent left her and went to go find Akira or Jet; finding the king first. Jet was looking around frantically, running over to Vincent when he spotted him. "Vincent have you seen Aurica? I can't find her anywhere."

Vincent nodded. "She's in her room. She jumped off the balcony again, and now she's rather upset that her wings aren't cooperating with her."

Jet looked down at Vincent's words. Frowning, Vincent inquired, "King Jet? Is everything ok?"

Jet looked at him and evenly replied, "Everything is fine. Thank you for taking care of Aurica."

Jet walked away toward Aurica's room to check up on her. Vincent walked off the other way after standing there for a bit, thinking to himself, *"Everyone is so depressed lately, I'm not sure if I can make it to the end of this. I'm going to have to start taking action soon. I think I know what I'll start with to pass the time."*

Jet walked into Aurica's room after knocking and hearing a faint reply, he walked over to her bed and sat down. She was under the covers, but she crawled through them and bumped into Jet, who laughed a little and tried to find an opening for her to come out from under the layers of material. After she was out, she laid her head on his lap, and he ran his hand through her hair. "I heard from Vincent that you jumped off the balcony again, and he told me the reason you're doing it."

She tried to escape under the covers again, but he stopped her, chastising, "You're a dragon, not a mole."

She looked at him. "What's a mole? Is it something from Ariliria?"

He nodded and put his hand on her head again. "I'll teach you more about the Ariliria, but now isn't the time. No more changing the subject Aurica."

She sighed and lay back down. "I know it's my fault you that can't get your wings to work for you. If I weren't human, you wouldn't have this problem, and Raiko will probably have the same issues as well. But jumping off of the balcony isn't the way to do it. All you're doing is scaring everyone, and before long Vincent might just lock you in a cage, and I might help him if you keep this up! Please Aurica, for the sake of your mother and me; stop jumping off the balcony, please."

Aurica sat up and nodded. "I promise never to do it again, and I mean it this time. So please don't let Vincent lock me in a cage."

Jet laughed and hugged her. "It's ok. I don't think he actually would, he's just been having that look ever since you started doing this."

Part 10

Aurica and Zander

Aurica had met Zander several times, and they had grown closer, even though he was always training with Vincent. They were in the training hall when Aurica went in to find Vincent; she walked down the stairs as Vincent walked over to her. "What brings you here, Princess Aurica?"

She paused in front of him with a speculative gleam in her eyes. "You. I need you to take me somewhere because mom won't let me leave the castle alone anymore."

He looked over at Zander and then back to her. "We're training right now; does it have to be right this minute?"

She walked over to Zander and grabbed his arm. "Yes, it does, you're both coming with me."

Vincent shrugged. "As you wish, Princess. Zander, we'll train later."

Zander nodded with a smile and they left, with Aurica and Zander walking ahead of Vincent. Watching the two together, Vincent thought, *'This may work better after all, I never thought of using him in this way...'*

Formulating a plan in his head, Vincent asked, "Princess, where are we going?"

Aurica looked back at him with a grin. "The dragons nest. I've wanted to go back for a while now."

They were going through the town when Zander saw Micah and Aria outside. He forgot he was holding Aurica's hand, and he ran after them, dragging her with him. After they reached the couple, Vincent hit zander on the head lightly, admonishing, "You shouldn't drag the Princess."

Zander blushed and apologized to Aurica, but she just laughed a little and turned to Micah and Aria who were waiting for them. Smiling brightly, Aria offered, "Princess Aurica, it's a pleasure to meet you! And it's nice to see you as well, Zander and Vincent."

Vincent nodded with a smile, while Zander went up to Aria and hugged her as Aurica said, "It's nice to meet you too, are you Zander's adoptive parents?"

They both nodded, and Aria had her arms around Zander as he turned toward Aurica and Vincent with a huge smile on his face.

Micah asked Vincent to go with him to talk, while Aria took the kids inside after getting the okay from Vincent. Micah and Vincent went to the tree on the hill; the one they went to during Vincent's last visit to talk, as it was a special place to them. It had become even more important now. Micah had proposed to Aria just a week and a half ago, and it was one of the things he wanted to talk to Vincent about. Crossing his arms, Micah said, "Zander looks great. I can tell you haven't been taking it easy on him; it's made him stronger."

Vincent turned around, and after a moment he smiled. "Me, take it easy on someone? Never going to happen, but you are right; it has made him much stronger. He doesn't talk about his mother much anymore, but I'm sure if he were alone with you or Aria that'd be a different story."

Micah looked at the town and smiled. "You know I've asked her to marry me and she said yes. You're coming to the wedding; it's not a request, as I'm sure you know."

Vincent went up to him and put his arm around Micah's neck in a brotherly way. "Like I'd have it any other way! It's about time, though; I thought I was going to get married before you two at this rate."

He got hit for that, of course, but then they started walking back together. "When are you going to get a girlfriend anyway? You can't get married without a significant other."

Vincent laughed and simply said, "All in good time, I've already made my choice."

Micah tried to find out who Vincent had chosen, but Vincent was a hard nut to crack; Micah gave up before they got to the house.

Aurica was having such a great time that she forgot about wanting to go to the dragon's nest, and before they knew it, Vincent and Micah were back. Vincent went up to Aurica first, looking at Aria as he said, "I should take Aurica back to the castle, as it's getting rather late."

Aurica frowned and tried to run to Aria, but Vincent caught her. "Princess Aurica, we can come back some other time. I saw guards outside looking for you just now. You didn't tell anyone where we were going, did you?"

She shook her head. "I did, but we came here instead, remember?"

He had forgotten too. "Regardless, we need to leave. Zander, you can stay here, as it's been awhile after all."

Aurica was trailing behind Vincent for most of the way; she wanted to stay with Micah and Aria a while longer, and couldn't understand why her guard was so uncompromising about the situation. *'He sure has been more on edge than he usually is; I wonder what's wrong...'*

When Vincent suddenly stopped for a group of people walking by, Aurica walked into him, but he didn't say anything except, "Aurica, stay there. It's best not to draw attention right now."

She remained where he'd told her to and waited for him to say it was ok to walk again. He looked back at her. "Ok, we can continue now. I know you're upset, but you're still my responsibility until Zander is older, and even after that, my duty is to the royal family. I've worked too hard to get in trouble for this."

The walk through the town was uneventful, but Vincent wasn't in a good mood for some reason, and Aurica didn't know what to say to him to cheer him up. She was eight and didn't have enough experience with him being like this, so she thought it might be a good idea to ask Phykira to talk to him instead. They passed several townspeople, who bowed to Aurica. She had been deep in thought but noticed them and started waving and smiling. Vincent just kept walking. He was getting more and more aggravated as each minute passed, but he was good at hiding it. *'Why couldn't she stay small enough for me to easily pick her up?'*

He kept walking ahead, periodically stopping and waiting for her to catch up, until they got to the castle, where Vincent asked another solider to walk Aurica to her room, and to her surprise, two went with her. They had gotten back much later than Vincent had expected to, and he still had to report to the captain, and then go back and get Zander.

Aurica went to her room, climbed onto the bed and tried to go to sleep, but found her thoughts keeping her awake. '*I want to know what's got him so upset! Maybe I really should ask Phykira to talk to him. She'll know what to do.*'

Instead of waiting for morning, she snuck over to Phykira's room. She didn't have trouble with the guards; she knew the castle and all the secret passage ways. Phykira wasn't sleeping. As a full dragon she didn't need to sleep as much as Aurica did; their rooms were more for privacy than anything else. Aurica was crawling through the vent shaft, muttering, "I'm going to have to find a new way soon…"

Her words trailed off as she reached the end of the shaft and heard Phykira talking to Vincent.

"Vincent, will you stay with me forever?"

He had been staring out her window, but he turned around and walked over to her. "Of course I will Phykira. Forever and always; as long as you want me."

She smiled and hugged him. "I'll always want you. I wonder if we could run away together, I'm sure it's going to be Aurica that Ignis chooses, so there is no point in me staying here."

He put his hand on her cheek. "We can if you really want to, but let's wait until after the ceremony."

She nodded and held him close again. When she put her head to his chest, he looked up at the vent where Aurica was hiding. He couldn't see her, but he knew she was there.

Panicking as he glanced to the vent where she was hiding, Aurica backed away and left. '*I didn't see that coming! I don't want her to leave, and I guess he'll just have to become a prince, because she will surely be chosen.*'

~~~~~~~

Jet was pacing around the throne room as Aurica and Raiko walked into the room, so they stopped and patiently waited for him to notice them. Normally Aurica would tackle him, but she wanted to set a good example for Raiko. She was also almost nine now and she had had high expectations placed upon her… not that she ever attempted to live up to them.

The ceremony where Ignis would choose their new ruler from one of the heirs was only two years away, but that wasn't why Jet was pacing. When it seemed like he was never going to notice them, they moved closer, with Aurica questioning, "Father? What's wrong?"

Jet stopped and blushed at his daughter's question, demanding, "How long have you two been standing there? Never mind... I need to go to Ariliria, and while Rayne is willing to take me, I want your mother to go with me as well. A couple of years ago we went there, and... Well, I found a surprise waiting for me and I want her to be there with me when I talk to him."

"To who?" Raiko asked, puzzled.

Shaking his head, Jet replied, "Maybe I'll tell you two one day, but for now it stays between your mother and me."

Disappointed that their father wouldn't confide in them, they followed him around the castle to find Akira. It took them awhile to find her, as she was running around the castle trying to find things she needed to help the townspeople. The guards had been traveling with her, but Akira had ordered them to stop following her when they kept getting in her way. Jet and the children split up to find her faster, but Jet ran into her first.

Akira's face was filled with worry as she said, "Jet! I was looking for you, but I was called away... I can't go with you this time, my love. My people need me right now, but Rayne can still take you there."

Jet nodded, disappointed that she wasn't going with him, but forced himself to smile and reassure her that her place was with her citizens. Wrapping his arms around her as she wilted in relief, Jet was forced to push back a thread of jealousy aimed at the Azelians. It wasn't their fault their planet was unstable, and the absence of their queen would only make it worse. Meeting his wife's eyes, he said, "Go help your people, Akira. We'll make the journey together another time."

"You're too good to me, Jeticous." Hugging her husband tightly, Akira took a moment to rest her head against his chest, relaxing further to the steady beat of his heart. Aurica and Raiko found them still standing in an embrace several minutes later, and looking down at them with a smile, Jet then met Akira's gaze, excitement shining on his face as he said, "I could take them with me... Would that be ok?"

After a brief hesitation in which she studied her daughter, Akira finally nodded, adding, "Just be careful, Aurica....mind your father."

Aurica made a pouty face. "Why are you only saying that to me? Raiko's going too!"

Jet laughed under his breath and she glared at him. Opening his arm to pull the children close, Jet leaned down to his daughter, whispering, "Your mother knows you well, girl."

Sighing as she watched her mother slip out of her father's arms to begin issuing orders once more, Aurica muttered, "Indeed."

~~~~~~~

Jet was packing the things that he and the children would need for the trip to Ariliria, worried that he'd forget something important. Rayne would have to be more careful with Raiko; the boy wasn't weak, but this was his first time making the journey. Aurica was running around after Raiko as they waited, trying to keep her brother entertained, while Akira was helping the people of the lower town.

Vincent had been looking for them and found them as they were getting on Rayne; the guard looking a little annoyed as he questioned, "Where are all of you going, King Jeticous?"

Aurica looked down at him, wondering why he cared. She looked around for Phykira, hoping that her sister would see that Vincent was being aggravated by the strangest things. Jet began to slide down from Rayne's back, replying, "We're going to Ariliria for a visit. Why, is something wrong?"

Vincent shook his head, but still looked annoyed. Jet looked confused, but he settled back down into position on the dragon's back, giving Rayne the silent signal that Akira had taught him years before. Nodding to the irritated guard as the large wings began to move, Jet tightened his hold on his children, and in a flash, they took off into the heavens.

Raiko didn't show much outward emotion, but inside he was excited about the trip. Aurica was very happy to go back to Ariliria, but she was also interested in finding out who her father was looking for. Jet continued to grow more and more nervous as they drew closer to Ariliria, and it seemed that they took longer to get there this time.

Because Jet was human, he had to be in a breathing and gravity system that moved and conformed to his body. Rayne was taking the journey slowly, gliding through space as the others were looking at the distant galaxies, glancing back at their solar system and then peering eagerly forward as they saw Ariliria's solar system come into view. They had just passed the outer planets when an asteroid hurtled by them with no warning.

His eyes wide, Raiko exclaimed, "Whoa that was close! Where did it come from?"

Jet looked back at the quickly disappearing hunk of rock, and then toward the biggest planet in the solar system, eyeing it speculatively. Nodding as he realized what had happened, he pointed to it, saying, "That's Jupiter, a gas giant, which has been called the "big brother" of Ariliria. It has long been known to throw asteroids and meteors away from the inner planets, and has even consumed them."

Narrowing his eyes at his father's words, Raiko nodded slowly as he absorbed the information, then asked, "What was the planet with the rings around it that we passed?"

Jet smiled at his son's curiosity. "That's my favorite, Saturn. There is debate about how the rings got there, but the one that makes the most sense; at least to me, is that a large asteroid, or perhaps a few smaller ones and a meteor, were pulled into Saturn's orbit, and were then crushed by the planet's gravity, and that's how the rings were made, but they are still doing research. They've found that many of the planets have rings, but they're just dimmer and slimmer, making them more difficult to see. After Jupiter is Mars, so once we get past Jupiter you'll be able to see it."

Aurica stood and tried to climb onto Rayne's head, but when the dragon let out a small growl, Jet grabbed his daughter and pulled her in front of him, chastising,. "Aurica, just be patient! Now sit still or you'll fall. Hey Raiko, you should scoot up here to see better."

Raiko nodded and slowly made his way to his father's back and held on. It took some time to get around Jupiter, as its gravity was incredibly strong, and though Rayne had flown by it before, she still wasn't used to its pull. Once around it, they saw Mars looming before them, with Ariliria a mere dot of light in the distance. The planets weren't aligned, but were at a distance where scientists could launch something toward it, as Ariliria's orbit was slightly faster, creating a whip-like effect.

"That's Mars?" The wonder in the boy's tone had Jet smiling as he nodded, shifting slightly so that Raiko could look around him to see it. "Scientists have sent rovers to mars, and they've found that it could've been just like Ariliria, but it doesn't have an iron core like Ariliria does. Its atmosphere was knocked out by solar energy over billions of years, and this is the result. However, they found ice on the side of a cliff, and where there is ice there is water; and where there is water there could be life."

"Do the dragon planets have iron cores?"

Jet shrugged. "I don't know, that is something you'd have to ask your mother or Ignis."

Aurica looked back out at the planets. "It looks like a blue marble."

Jet laughed. "People have often called it that, Aurica, because it is so beautiful. But, it hasn't always been called Ariliria. There were a series of wars; wars that used massively destructive weapons that changed the continents on the planet and killed many, many people. When peace was finally declared, nothing looked the same, so the people decided that they needed a change to match their planet, and the planet of Ariliria was born."

Shaken by his father's talk of war, Raiko looked around again to see Ariliria, only to find that they were still passing Mars, and with a frown, questioned, "Dad? Is Mars smaller than Ariliria?"

Jet looked back at Raiko and nodded. "Yes, it is, good observation son."

Raiko smiled as Jet shifted him and put him in front of Aurica so that he was in a better position to see. Aurica was a little irritated, but then she just decided to let it go, asking, "What are the planets past Ariliria?"

Enjoying the science lesson with his children, Jet replied, "The one after it is Venus; which is the hottest planet, and after that is Mercury."

Raiko studied the dots of light in the distance and then back at Jet, a frown on his face as he queried, "How is Venus hotter than Mercury? Shouldn't Mercury be hotter?"

"I guess it's good that I paid attention to astronomy in school, or I would think the same thing. Mercury doesn't have an atmosphere, so there is nothing to keep the heat there. Venus, on the other hand, has a thick atmosphere; even thicker than Ariliria's, which absorbs the heat and prevents it from escaping. It's hot enough on the surface to melt tin and lead."

Aurica and Raiko both looked at the planets with amazement, thinking about how similar, and yet so different, this solar system was from their own. Rayne had to increase her speed to make the approach to Ariliria. The dragon had been to Ariliria many times, and knew that she had to have enough speed for the safest entry into the planet's atmosphere, and she had been reserving energy for this very reason.

As they made their approach to Ariliria's outer orbit, the proximity lights of the satellites flashed around them, and as they moved even closer, they saw the space junk that circled the planet, noting that it wasn't a pretty sight. Shaking her head at the mess, Aurica asked, "Dad, why is there so much junk circling the Ariliria?"

Noting the displeasure in his daughter's voice, Jet explained, "It's from sending things out of our orbit, and from satellites colliding with each other, or extraterrestrial objects impacting them... Among other things."

Wrapping his arms around the children as Rayne found the site where they could enter undetected, Jet enjoyed the sight of his home world once more, and after looking around to insure that it was safe, allowed the dragon to land. She decided to stay there instead of leaving, but some of the people and the animals nearby had already seen her, and with a sigh, she was forced to camouflage herself as her passengers hurried out of the clearing.

They were sneaking through the forest, with the kids playing in the trees, as Jet stopped and watched a young couple holding hands at their wedding. A tear ran down his face and he quickly wiped it away before the kids noticed. Aurica, though, had seen the surreptitious action and immediately went still, watching her father. After several seconds she walked over to Jet and asked him what was going on. With a sigh, he slowly turned to her and explained, "Those two people have decided to live their lives together; we call it getting married. Your mother and I married in that tradition, and I was just recalling our wedding day."

The young man looked a lot like Jet, with dark hair and green eyes, and he was tall and slender. The woman had red hair and green eyes, and was of medium height and slender. The man suddenly looked back at the brush curiously, but when his wife drew his attention back to her, he smiled happily and they looked at each other tenderly before linking hands and walking on through the forest. Jet still had tears in his eyes, making his children wonder if they should leave him for a bit. He suddenly stood, whispered for them to stay there, and ran off in the direction the couple had gone.

The newlyweds went into a building at the edge of the village, the man returning after only a minute. As he exited, he saw Jet, and smiling as he walked past the older man, whispered "Thanks for coming. I'm glad to see you're well."

Wind dragons

Plain in appearance, they make up for in their ability to control the wind. They have feathers around their wrists and ankles, they can force these feathers off and send them traveling at high speeds. However; this causes damage to them with each use. They are peaceful and non-aggressive, making these feathers obsolete and more decorations than anything. They provide loyalty and embrace freedom.

The wind dragon humanoids, white to light lime green or blue hair, lime or yellow eyes, typically light skinned.

Planet name: Gustavas

Part II

The Time Dragon Appears

For the longest time, it felt like they were being followed. It wasn't a familiar presence, so they knew it wasn't Vincent or Phykira, but the sensation was there all the same. It seemed to increase when whoever, or whatever, this was, was inching closer. Kairi was acting strangely too, as though she feared whatever it was. They were in a dense forest, when Aurica decided that she'd had enough; it was time to call this person out and end the ridiculous game of hide and seek. Turning to face the direction of where she felt the presence, she yelled, "Ok this ends now, come out!"

Her eyes widened when a man walked out from behind a tree wearing strange garments none of them had seen before. Pausing several feet away, he met Aurica's gaze as he said, "I'm just going to get this out of the way. I'm a time dragon; one of the last ones that you could tame. I am here to tell you that I will not join you, or even think about it, until you locate all of the other dragons. You seem too young and too reckless to me, to tell the truth."

They were all stunned by his words, but Aurica refused to allow that to interfere with her quest. Straightening her back, she stepped closer to him, stating, "I will prove you wrong, and you will find yourself joining me on my quest."

The new-found dragon smirked at her and moved even closer. "You can try, little girl, but I won't make things easy for you. You and your friends think that you are so smart; so ready to take on the universe, but you have no idea what I've already done for you."

Curious, she looked at him with a new fascination, demanding, "What do you mean?"

He stepped back with another smirk and turned around, replying, "Your enemy has nearly found you here several times. I keep leading him away; but he's starting to notice that the trail always disappears in the vicinity of this planet. It won't be long until he comes back."

Aurica tensed at his words, too focused on the new information to ask who was behind her attempted kidnapping and the destruction of Azelia.

At her silence the time dragon turned back around. "I think I'll travel with you for a while, but don't get the wrong idea though."

She nodded with a smile and they continued to walk toward their next destination. *This is great! Mom said that I shouldn't count on any dragons even confronting me, but this one did. I wonder why, though? I thought time dragons hated fire dragons, but maybe he's rogue or something.*

The time dragon walked behind them most of the way, wondering, *'Where are they even heading to? There are no dragons out this way, and I could tell her that, but this is more entertaining.*

Aurica knew that there were no dragons in the direction they were heading, but she still had a feeling that they should continue moving away from the area where they'd found the time dragon.

Somewhere along the way Raiko and Kairi went missing, and the others quickly turned around to go look for them, splitting into two groups. Aurica, Calcifer, Zander, Conrad and the time dragon went one way, while Enki, Rikku, Aquilo, Damini and Anahita went another. Though the time dragon was looking around, as though he were assisting in the search, Aurica knew that he wasn't really looking for Raiko and Kairi. He had been acting strangely right before they disappeared, and she was beginning to wonder if he'd had something to do with it. He didn't remain with her for long; something seemed to be bothering him, so she wasn't surprised when he took off.

When her team met back up with the others, she told them of her suspicions about the time dragon and the disappearance of their friends, and the others seemed to share her opinion. Aquilo, Enki and Anahita volunteered to search for the missing dragon, with Damini and Rikku joining them. Watching as her best friend disappeared into the forest with the dragons that had bound themselves to her, Aurica could only hope that the time dragon didn't do something to them as well. Sighing as she turned back to her remaining companions, Aurica weighed her options. While she wanted to back track to find Raiko and Kairi, she hated the thought of the wasted time, but she couldn't leave her younger brother and his friend out there to fend for themselves. Though she had a bad feeling about retracing their steps, Aurica turned back towards their last camp, with her friends falling in around her. Casting glances her way as they followed their own trail through the forest; they realized that while she was far from happy about the situation, for her younger brother, she'd do anything.

~~~~

Vincent was becoming frustrated with everything that had had gone wrong, and that he still couldn't locate Aurica. He had brainwashed Phykira to help him find Aurica, but she could no longer sense her. He didn't like having to keep her brainwashed, but when he had originally captured her she had been sad, angry and wanted to kill him, so he felt like he had no choice; not only for his safety, but for hers as well. Phykira seemed to slowly be getting over the brainwashing, as she subconsciously started calming down and accepting what had happened. Vincent's younger brother, Klaus, was getting irritated too. He wanted to land on another planet so that he could flirt with some girls. He didn't care that much about finding Aurica, even though he knew that locating the girl was his brothers' current goal.

"Klaus, stop pacing; it's getting annoying!" Klaus stopped, but then he started tapping the control panel repeatedly. "I can't help it brother, I'm bored out of my mind. Let's just land on an inhabited planet with pretty girls. We'll find Aurica eventually; she's going to be looking for the dragons she needs, so let's just track *their* energies."

Vincent turned to stare at his brother, surprised by the simplistic genius of the suggestion. "That's a brilliant idea! We'll track down the dragon presences from different worlds, and somewhere in the mix, we'll find the brat."

As Vincent turned around to enter in new search parameters; Klaus rolled his eyes and wandered off.

Phykira walked in a little while after Klaus left, stating, "Vincent, I can feel Aurica's presence again."

He stood up and went over to her, holding her eyes with his as he demanded, "Where is she?"

She walked past him and went to the space map that had the nearby planets and stars, pointing at a blue planet as she answered, "This one, Ariliria."

Vincent rushed over and plotted the course to Ariliria. After entering the coordinates, he turned back around to praise Phykira, and found her just standing there with her arms on her head. Crossing to her, he softly asked, "Phykira, are you okay?"

Removing her hands from her head, she sighed, answering, "I'm fine. It's just that Aurica is much stronger now and it's hurting my head. I... I think she can sense that I've found her."

Vincent put his arm around Phykira's shoulders and led her to his room. The course for Ariliria was already set, so he didn't have to be in the control room. Easing the princess down onto the bed, he gently rubbed her shoulders until she began to relax and then slowly drifted off to sleep.

Once Phykira was asleep, Vincent left to find Klaus, annoyed when he found him snooping in the hold. It only took Vincent a minute to realize that Klaus was trying to find a way to get to a planet; any planet, without Vincent or Phykira. Leaning against the door, he drawled, "You know, escape capsules won't get you very far, right? You won't be able to get off of whatever backwards planet you land on, and I won't come save you. Phykira's found Aurica. She's on a populated planet, so just be patient and you'll have enough girls to flirt with for the rest of your life."

He turned away, knowing that his brother wouldn't think about doing anything stupid for now, but it wouldn't last long. Klaus was satisfied with his brother's words, and confirmed Vincent's thoughts when he suddenly demanded, "Wait... When will we be getting to that planet?"

Vincent was still nearby, but he didn't feel like turning around, instead calling, "Seeing as Phykira can now sense her strongly enough to cause a headache, and that I have the ship moving at full speed, it shouldn't be very long. A week, at the very least."

He continued walking, ignoring Klaus' growl of impatience. Wincing as Vincent slammed the door behind him, Klaus decided it might be a good idea to stop bothering Vincent before he got hurt, or the other man decided to jettison him in one of the pods he'd been examining...

~~~

It had been several days since Phykira had sensed Aurica, and Aurica now sensed Phykira as well. She tried to get through to her sister, but the other girl's mind was clouded, and after that, she closed the link between them. Phykira told Vincent what happened, and he knew that Aurica was now going to be much harder to find. "We'll split up. Klaus isn't going to be a lot of help, so it'll just be you and me looking for Aurica."

Klaus walked in on Vincent's statement, and smiling, declared, "I'll help; I just want to have some fun first. Think about it, I'm social, likeable and can get information. Aurica was, and still is, just a kid. People are bound to notice a child traveling alone, and try to help her by contacting others."

Phykira shook her head. "She's not alone; Zander and Conrad are with her."

Vincent wasn't worried about either of them; he had trained Zander himself, and knew Conrad's fighting style. He had always been stronger than both of them, and he didn't think that they could get much stronger on their own. "After nearly four years of searching for her, I'm not going to let that stop me."

The blue planet quickly came into view. Not a lot had happened during this last part of their journey, but they were all very anxious, especially Vincent. He knew that not having Azelia around would make it harder to get Aurica to agree to his plan, but he did have her sister, and he planned on taking Zander as another hostage before attempting to capture Aurica. He had thought about snagging Conrad as well, but he wasn't sure that he could handle both of them in the ship he had. Raiko was also a target if he needed a larger bargaining chip, as Aurica would do anything for Raiko. The boy would also be the easiest to snatch if he wasn't with Aurica, and Phykira hadn't said anything about Raiko when she'd felt Aurica's presence.

They passed by the satellites and their information was taken in by the ship. Glancing at the data, he said, "Hey Klaus, look."

He wanted his brother to get his flirting out of the way, and the satellite data had images and broadcasts, many of them featuring young women. Perking up at what he was seeing, Klaus, commented, "Oh nice! Some of these human girls are actually pretty, and I know you want me to help, but I have my own business to attend to. I'll keep an eye out for Aurica and listen for any information, but I have to take care of me first, ya know? Good luck brother."

He took off running and went to a docking port that allowed them to leave the ship while still in the air. It was big enough for dragons, he quickly donned a protective suit and jumped from the open hatch, his screams of excitement filling the comms system.

After Klaus left they waited until they were a little closer to their destination and then did the same. Once they reached the ground Phykira tried to sense Aurica, but she was shutting Phykira out and not allowing a telepathic link. Phykira could still feel her presence, but it wasn't precise. They decided to go to the place Phykira had felt her last and go from there.

"Maybe you should search for Raiko first, Phykira." Phykira stopped and tried to sense Raiko, and as he wasn't shutting Phykira out, she was able to find him easily. Turning to Vincent with a smile, she said, "He's not far; he sensed me and is coming to us."

Vincent thought about it for a moment and quickly hatched a new plan. "Phykira, you travel with Raiko and find Aurica; I'll follow you."

She nodded and tried to sense Raiko again, finding that he was almost to their location. Satisfaction filling him at the news, Vincent hid himself, smirking as the gullible young boy fell into their trap.

~~~

Klaus immediately found a beach and landed far enough away that no one saw him. He ran as fast as he could, running into a girl who then dropped her purse, sending her things flying. She had brown hair, blue eyes, jean capris and a white tank top on. She hadn't had the best day, but she remained calm and started picking up her things. Klaus helped her, offering, "Hey, I'm so sorry! I wasn't watching where I was going. I'm Klaus, what's your name?"

After they finished picking up her possessions, they looked at each other, and they both blushed. Dropping her eyes, she said, "My name is Casey, it's nice to meet you, Klaus. Thanks for helping me pick up my things."

She started walking toward him, but tripped and fell into him, blushing in embarrassment. Watching the red tinge her cheeks, Klaus questioned, "Hey, are you alright? Casey?"

He had his hands on her shoulders, and as she tried to stand up straight, he supported her with an arm around her shoulders. Grimacing in pain as she looked down at her ankle, she answered, "Thanks, Klaus, I think I hurt my ankle; I hate to ask you this after just meeting you, but could you carry me over to a chair?"

Klaus didn't even give her an answer before he picked her up, causing her to blush once more and clutch her bag to her stomach. He found an empty chair and sat her down gently, thinking, '*It's at times like this that I wish I had healing powers. It's my fault that she got hurt, so I'll stay with her for a bit to see if she needs help, it's the least I can do.*'

Casey situated herself where she could take the pressure off of her ankle and look at it, while Klaus took her purse and set it on a table next to her. Smiling, he said, "Well, I'm at your service, Casey; it's payback for me running into you."

She was fine with that, and as she smiled her acceptance, he sat next to her chair and they talked for a long time. She had just gotten out of a relationship the previous day, and everything else that could possibly go wrong had seemed to follow. She, of course, asked him what he was doing. "I'm looking for my little sister. Her name is Aurica; have you seen her?"

Casey sat up too fast and tried to stand on the ankle she had hurt. Catching her trembling form, Klaus helped her to sit back down, soothing, "Hey, hey take it easy."

"What are you doing here with me if you're looking for your younger sister? She could be hurt, or worse!"

He laughed and sat back down. "Its fine, our brother is out looking for her too, and to be honest, he's a lot better at tracking her down. She's not lost though; she ran away from home after she got into a fight with our brother."

She calmed down and relaxed into the chair again. "Don't scare me like that! This is a dangerous place, especially for kids."

"Not that you're a kid, but that's even more reason for me to stay with you, considering I've made it harder for you to walk. Just let me know when you want me to carry you home... And I promise that I'm not a creep."

She giggled and looked at him. "I wouldn't have let you carry me the first time if I thought you were. I should have you take me home now so that you can help in the search for your sister. I wish that I could help, but I'd just be a huge hindrance at this point. She has a very pretty name by the way."

He nodded with a smile; and grabbing her purse, Casey indicated that she was ready for him to pick her up. Just as he was about to lift her in his arms, Aurica walked by. At least he thought it was her, but he had honestly never seen her. He only knew her from the description that Vincent had given him; reddish brown hair and red eyes. As he watched he noticed that she kept looking around, as though searching for something, and he realized that the boy was not with her. She must have been searching for Raiko when she wound up there.

Following his gaze, Casey saw the flash of bright hair as a young girl crossed the street, and drawing his attention back to her, asked, "Is that Aurica? That girl had reddish brown hair, what color are her eyes?" When he didn't reply, she prompted "Klaus? Is everything ok?"

He looked back to Casey and put his hand on his head. "Sorry about that, I thought I saw my sister."

Casey looked around again, over-looking Aurica because of her hair color. Klaus acted like he, too, was looking again, but he kept his eyes on Aurica. *'Come on just turn around! If that is Aurica, what should I do? If I were her brother, I would've recognized her right away, and of course, if I went up to her she wouldn't look confused or freaked out. I should just take Casey home, and then come back and find this girl if she doesn't turn around soon.'*

~~~~

When Calcifer had mentioned to Aurica that he could hear the thoughts of someone who was looking for her; she drew power from Enki to change her eye color to brown, hoping that would offer some protection from the person searching for her. *'Damnit, where could Raiko be, and who here would be looking for me? Maybe one of my enemies henchmen; that would explain why that time dragon was on edge.'*

~*~

She turned to where Klaus could see her eyes. 'Nope not her, she has brown eyes. Time to bring Casey home and continue the search my way. He picked Casey up without much warning and he carried her away. "Which way to your house my lady?"

Laughing softly, Casey replied, "Keep going this way good sir."

They both laughed and he brought her home safely, reluctantly parting on the premise of needing to search for his sister.

~*~

Raiko and Kairi arrived at the clearing Raiko had been drawn to, but they both had a bad feeling, so they approached Phykira cautiously. Raiko couldn't help himself, running up to Phykira when he got close enough. Vincent was watching and when he saw Kairi, murmured, "It seems Raiko made a little friend... We'll have to get her to leave or we'll have to take her too."

Phykira was still hugging Raiko as tears coursed down her cheeks. She might be brainwashed, but she wasn't so far out of it that she didn't know her brother or remember how much she missed him. Kairi moved closer after they stopped hugging, offering, "Hi, I'm Kairi, Raiko's friend."

Phykira turned to her, as did Raiko. He felt bad for not introducing them, but Kairi knew it had been awhile. A lifetime of royal etiquette filled Phykira, and holding out her hand, she replied, "Nice to meet you Kairi, I'm Raiko's older sister, Phykira. Have you two seen Aurica? I need to find her."

Raiko and Kairi looked at each other, and then back to the older girl, with Raiko finally replying. "Yeah, we're traveling with them but we were just taking a walk and got lost. We can probably find them with your help."

As they set off to search for Aurica together, Kairi felt uncomfortable around her friend's sister, but for Raiko's sake, she didn't say anything. Vincent was happy when they finally set off, as he was quickly getting tired of sitting around. He wanted Kairi to leave, but since it didn't look like she was going to, he figured that he and Phykira would have to grab both of the children right before they got to Aurica.

On their way, they ran into two travelers; a young girl and boy; and found themselves surprised when the girl stopped and was staring at Phykira. Realizing that she'd been caught, the girl apologized, "I'm sorry, but you look like someone I know, my mistake."

Phykira was confused at first, but became hopeful as she demanded, "Who? I'm looking for my younger sister, so maybe she's the one you're thinking of. Her name is Aurica."

The girl looked shocked. "Yes, Aurica! You're her sister? I haven't seen her for a couple of years, but you two look so much alike."

Phykira just smiled. She'd known that someone was bound to notice the resemblance between them. Vincent had also relied on that fact.

Raiko suddenly felt Aurica's presence and contacted her, asking her where she was. Aurica didn't give her location, but immediately set out to find him, telling him to stay where he was. Raiko let everyone know the news that Aurica was on her way with the others, and Phykira wasn't sure what to do, so she said that she needed to go into the forest to think about what to say to Aurica.

Phykira hurried into the nearby trees, and after she looked around to make sure that no one had followed her, hissed, "Vincent!"

When Vincent came out of hiding, he already knew what was going on, and was trying to think of a strategy. There were so many of them, and he didn't want to hurt anyone, but his excuse for being nice was that there would be more hostages for him to take if Aurica needed any encouragement to do his bidding. "I think you should go back out there, greet Aurica like the sister you haven't seen in years, and I will continue to wait for the right moment. Try to get them away from at least those newcomers; the fewer witnesses, the better."

She nodded and took off; seeing that Aurica had just arrived as Phykira returned to where the others were waiting. Vincent almost ran out there himself when he spotted the young queen, but as he moved to reveal himself, Klaus showed up and stopped him, saying, "You should listen to your own advice brother. Now is not the time."

Vincent nodded, and they turned to wait.

Aurica immediately knew that there was something wrong with Phykira, but she was happy to see her. Phykira was also happy to see Aurica, but frowned when her younger sister asked, "Sister, it's so good to see you! But… Why were your thoughts cloudy?"

Phykira thought for a moment. "I'm not sure. I didn't realize my thoughts were cloudy, but I have had a terrible headache lately… And I was wondering why you shut me out."

Aurica felt bad, but she knew her gut feeling had been right, and shutting her sister out had been the right thing to do. Turning, she saw Cecelia, and with a bright smile, declared, "This is great! I was looking for you too, and now we've found each other."

Cecelia was still impressed by how much they looked alike. She and her sister didn't look much alike, but until recently she hadn't seen very much of the world. She was amazed that two people could look so much alike and not be twins.

After several minutes of talking, Cecelia and her companion said that they had to take off, and Aurica told her that she would be sure to catch up with her later.

Vincent was happy when they finally left, because he and Klaus were getting tired of waiting around on a group of chatty teens. Vincent used a remote signal to call for the ship to come to their location. He didn't care about the plan he'd made anymore, he would just get them all at once and be done with it, and now that Klaus was back with him, he knew that he could handle all of them. The ship hadn't been far away, and he could already see it growing on the horizon. Turning to his brother, he ordered, "Now Klaus. Use your dome barrier and have it enclose them."

Klaus did just that, enjoying the look on their faces as everyone other than Phykira was enclosed in a black see-through dome. Not sure what was going on, they all gathered around Aurica to protect her, with both Conrad and Zander shouting, "What's going on? Aurica stay in the middle!"

They continued to look around, trying to figure out what was happening, when Aurica noticed that Vincent and Klaus were walking out of the forest. They all tensed at the appearance of the men, and as the dome continued to get smaller and smaller; until there was hardly any room for them to move, they knew that the presence of the guard and the stranger wasn't good news.

Vincent and Klaus walked to the edge of the dome, and crossing his arms over his chest, Vincent taunted, "It's so nice to see all of you again! And Aurica; your highness, I've been looking for you everywhere. Seems like you've grown a bit from when I last saw you, but that's not important. Now, come with me, or I'll kill all of your friends one by one."

He held out his hand with a smirk on his face, and Phykira went to his side. "Aurica, do as he says, you know he'll make good on his threats."

Calcifer, Conrad, Zander and Raiko refused to step aside or let Aurica through, and Kairi remained as close to Aurica as a shadow. Vincent began to lose his patience, and Klaus made the top middle section of the dome collapse inward, taking the form of a doughnut and leaving Aurica and Kairi exposed while the boys were still trapped inside.

Klaus jumped over the twisted dome, grabbing them both, and then brought them over to Vincent and Phykira. He released Kairi, but kept a tight hold on Aurica, while Phykira grabbed Kairi so that she couldn't interfere. Vincent sauntered up to Aurica and Klaus, smug in his position even as Aurica continued struggling to get free; fighting harder as Vincent came closer and closer, but Klaus was too strong.

Vincent grabbed Aurica's face and pulled her closer to his. "Now this is more like it, however, since you did not come of your own free will, your friend's lives are now all in my hands. I suggest that you stop fighting and come quietly, or I can't guarantee that they'll make it out of this clearing alive."

Vincent looked at Klaus and gave him the signal to release her; the other man let Aurica go as Vincent stepped away as well. Taking his words to heart, Aurica was looking down at the ground and didn't move. Vincent turned and started walking away; Klaus went over to the dome and turned toward Aurica. "Well Aurica, what will you do? I will make this dome disappear if you do as my brother ordered."

Aurica looked up, glancing over toward them, and then at Vincent who had stopped. With a sigh, she started walking toward Vincent. Vincent's deep chuckle filled the glade as he said, "Good decision Aurica. For now keep them in that dome, Klaus; don't release them until we're all on the ship."

Aurica reached Vincent, who took her arm and started walking. Phykira was on his other side and Klaus was running over to catch up.

They boarded the ship, and Vincent took Aurica to a chamber he had made for her. "Klaus, you know what to do, I'll be back."

He released Aurica's arm and continued walking; she followed him. Vincent looked back periodically but Aurica kept her head down as she walked. Sighing at her attitude, Vincent said, "Don't look so down, Aurica, this is your fate. You have incredible power, but don't think that you can just keep it all to yourself."

She stopped dead in the middle of the corridor, causing him to do the same. Her eyes flashed with red flames as she growled, "My power will be used to restore my planet; my people. It's not for you and whatever it is you want."

He laughed. "That's almost the same thing I want. Now continue walking. I'll fill you in when we get to your room." She reluctantly started walking again and passed him, he followed her.

They were half way down a hall when he ordered, "Stop here."

Aurica stopped and turned around as Vincent went to the only door on that side of the hall, placing his hand in front of the door and saying, "Unlock."

There was a clicking sound and then it opened to reveal a windowless room. Turning to face her, Vincent said, "Only I can open this door, so don't think you can escape. Now go inside."

She walked to the doorway, and stopped, but Vincent pushed her in and she almost fell over. He closed the door behind them and locked it. Aurica looked around, and realizing that the room was huge and nice, she turned to face Vincent with a raised eyebrow. Vincent looked down at her, and putting his hand on her shoulder, turned her around and leaned toward her as he stated, "This room is sealed, and if you touch the walls, they will hurt you badly. I will come for you and take you where I want you for that day. Klaus has gone back down to Ariliria to find the rest of the dragons, because you're going to need them... I don't want you to die when you reform the time planet, after all."

She turned her head. "No. I will reform my planet."

He sighed and stood up, roughly grabbing her arm, noting that she was in pain but didn't make a sound or try to get away. "You don't have a choice in the matter, so be a good girl or I'll have to hurt you more."

He released her and then held out his hand in front of her; using his powers to send her flying toward the big bed in the middle of the room. "Go to sleep!"

A barrier surrounded the bed after she landed, trapping her in place. With no other option, she wearily closed her eyes and gave in to her exhaustion.

~~~~

Zander and the others were taken on the ship as well; where they were finally released from the dome, to find that Klaus was the only one with them in a giant room. They didn't try anything, as they weren't sure where Aurica and Kairi were and didn't want to jeopardize their safety. Phykira had taken Kairi to another room, and while it was not as nice as Aurica's, it was nicer than the giant room the boys were in. In the boys' room Klaus explained that Vincent had Aurica and that Kairi had been taken in as well. "I have other things to do, but I have to wait until Vincent gets back to seal this room."

Vincent walked in shortly after, ordering, "Klaus, get going."

After Klaus was out of the room, he left too and sealed the door behind him. Klaus hadn't taken off yet and was waiting for Vincent. "Brother, why did you have Phykira bring that human girl with us? We won't be coming back here after we find the other dragons, so shouldn't we release her? I can take her down; I have to go back there to find the dragons anyway."

Vincent faced him, his expression like granite as he replied, "No, the girl will stay here. Aurica and Raiko care for her, so she'll make a good hostage. You go find the dragons as I pinpoint their location from here. Oh, and you can take Phykira with you."

Klaus shook his head. "Nah, you have your hands full, so keep her here to help. I'll be back."

Phykira went into the control room and found Vincent plotting a course back to their solar system. Stopping beside him, she requested, "Can I go in Aurica's room? I want to talk to her."

He turned around in the chair and up stood, replying, "I'm busy, but sure, let's go."

They left and started walking toward Aurica's room when Vincent questioned, "How is that young girl doing? The one you brought here."

Neither of them looked at each other as she replied, "She's fine. She begged me to let her go and asked how I could do this to my own siblings. Other than that, I think she'll be okay."

He laughed and they kept walking.

They arrived at Aurica's room and Vincent unsealed the door to let Phykira in. Aurica was lying on the bed and didn't move, so Vincent closed the door after Phykira was in, and sealed it shut with Phykira inside, calling, "Phykira, I'll be back in a while."

With that, he left to track down the dragons. After he left, Aurica sat up, facing the wall, her back stiffening when Phykira sat down on the bed next to her. Aurica turned and stared at Phykira, startling her with the directness of her gaze. "You should not stare Aurica, it's rude. You know, I thought you were dead. The planet is gone and so is everyone else."

Aurica looked away and said in a spiteful tone, "If Vincent hadn't attacked, none of this would have happened, and we would still be happy."

Phykira looked away. "Happy? I wasn't happy. I had to wait for my siblings to get older just so I could get rejected. Vincent was the *only* one who ever understood me and cared for me. Just help Vincent, and then he'll let you stay on the new planet. He won't kill you; he knows I love you and never want you to get hurt."

Aurica rolled back to the other side "I won't help him, so he'll just have to kill me."

Phykira rolled her eyes. "Stop being stubborn and melodramatic, Aurica. He won't kill you; he'd kill Zander, Conrad and that little human girl first. One by one, just like he said."

Aurica rolled back over and sat up enraged. "No! If he's going to hurt anyone, it should be me. I'm the one who won't help him; the rest had nothing to do with this."

Phykira rose to her feet, admonishing, "Aurica don't be stupid! He needs you, so he won't kill you. Just do as he says, or he might even harm Raiko or me. Stop being selfish."

Phykira heard Vincent unsealing the door, so she walked over to the door where Vincent was waiting for her. The man's smirk was back in place as he said, "Listen to your sister, Aurica, many good things will come from your cooperation; but many more bad things will happen if you cross me."

Aurica lay back down and turned around, effectively rejecting his words. Vincent and Phykira left the room, and Vincent sealed the door again. Meeting Phykira's eyes, he said, "It won't come to me harming you or Raiko, I promise. I know that you were just trying to scare her, but it won't go that far."

Phykira looked at him and shrugged. "I know, I didn't mean to go that far with the threats, but... She was just irritating me."

Vincent laughed a bit. "Yes, she is frustrating, but she is the only one who can help. While there is another way, it would take a long time."

Phykira looked confused. "What is the other way?"

When he remained silent, she looked at his face and found that he was blushing. Shrugging at her inquisitive gaze, he explained, "Having children, but there is no guarantee."

Phykira looked down, now blushing herself. "Oh, I see. Well... that wouldn't be a bad thing to do."

They kept walking, and then Phykira went off down a different hall to her room.

~~~

Klaus returned for the day, dirty and exhausted. "Brother, I found the plant dragon, but she wouldn't come with me, she escaped."

Vincent wasn't pleased, but Klaus had used a lot of energy on the barrier he had created earlier and then changed its form and shape, which was very draining. "Tomorrow then. Go rest now, Klaus."

Klaus left and Vincent looked for more of the dragons. *I keep getting a strange blip on the radar, and I wonder what it could be. It has the same energies as the dragons, so It must be a powerful one; dark and light are both capable of concealing themselves; as are time…'*

Pushing the thought of his people away, he turned away and decided he would retire to his room as well.

~*~*

In the middle of the night, the time dragon that Aurica had encountered before appeared in her room. *'He'll have to do better than this to keep me out.'* He walked over to her, to find that she was sleeping quite soundly. Shaking his head, he murmured, "Aurica, this is the only time that I'll ever save you."

He picked her up; transporting out of the ship and to Ariliria. Ending up in a park, near a city she had been to before, he paused when he heard people coming. "You know this could have turned out much worse for you. If you get caught again, then maybe you *aren't* worthy; of course, you *are* still a child."

The people he heard were getting closer. *'They seem to be kind people. I'm sure they'll take care of her.'* He set her down and ran his fingers through her hair, thinking, *'Such a stubborn child, but I guess she could be worse though.'*

He stepped away and took off. The people he heard were a young couple, and when they saw Aurica; they panicked. The young man went to check on her while the woman called the police. "Hello! Please help! My boyfriend and I found a young girl who has collapsed in the park."

"We're sending someone, just stay there with her."

The girl hung up and went over to her boyfriend, who had picked Aurica up and was walking over to a bench to set her on, calling back to her, "She seems fine."

Worried, the young girl went over to them, and a few minutes later she noticed some lights in the parking lot of the park. Pointing them out to her boyfriend, he ran over to show them where the child was. "Over here. The young girl is over on that bench with my girlfriend."

The medics rushed past him, and the girl, who had seen them coming, was standing and made room for them. They checked Aurica for a moment and then put her on a stretcher and into an ambulance. The medics took off and the police stayed and asked them a couple questions. "Do you two know the girl? Did you see what happened?"

The girl shook her head. "No, we were just passing through. It's a short cut we take to get to his apartment, and we saw her and called the police right away. We didn't see anything or anyone else… I'm sorry we couldn't be of more help."

The officer shook his head. "There is no telling what could have happened if you two hadn't found her when you did. But don't worry; if we don't find her family, we'll take good care of her."

They nodded and left, the police following soon after.

~~~~

Vincent woke up, and as he had a bad feeling, he checked on Aurica and found that she was gone. Fury rushed through him, and turning around with a snarl, he hit the wall so hard that over half of it collapsed. Klaus was nearby and rushed over, thinking Vincent was going too far in threatening Aurica. "Brother, must you take things so far? Wait, where's Aurica?"

Vincent turned around in a rage. "That's what I would like to know. I'm the only one that can open this door, so how'd she escaped? Are the others still aboard?"

Klaus grimaced. "I'm not sure…" They both went together. Klaus was nervous, afraid that Vincent would hit him next if he became any angrier. When they got to the other holding room, everyone was there, looking concerned. "What was that noise, what did you do to Aurica?"

Vincent turned away. They didn't have anything to do with it. "Nothing, everything is fine, just remodeling the ship a bit."

Vincent left without another word; Klaus followed behind him.

Frowning at the once more sealed door, Zander stated, "That was weird; Vincent wouldn't come down here just to turn and walk away, saying something like that. That's a waste of energy and he would never do that."

Conrad nodded in agreement "You're right, Zander. You worked with him more than anyone, so what's with him?"

Zander looked down "I'm not sure. He's completely different, at least when compared to how he was at the castle. He was kind, stern and caring, not the soulless psychopath he seems to be now. I know that even if all of that changed, what he just did was strange and that would apply to others too, not many people would waste their time just for that."

They heard the door opening so they stopped talking, but it was just Phykira bringing Kairi to them. Raiko jumped up and ran to the door of the cell. Phykira smirked "You never get this excited to see me Raiko, I feel insulted. I'm getting tired of babysitting and hearing this girl talk, so it's your turn. I'll be back for her later."

She opened the cell door and pushed Kairi inside, and into Raiko's arms. "Why are you being so mean Phykira? I was happy to see you, until you turned on us. Why not just leave her here; it's not right for her to be all alone."

Phykira laughed. "Alone? Like I said I'm getting tired of babysitting her. She hasn't been alone for more than eight hours, and that was for sleep."

With those words, Phykira left, shutting and locking the door behind her.

Waiting until Phykira's footsteps faded away, Conrad turned to Calcifer, demanding, "Where's Aurica? Do you still have your bond with her?"

A slow, satisfied smile filled the dragon's face, and with a simple nod, he replied, "She's safe."

~~~~

Vincent was still pacing and wondering not only about how Aurica was able to escape, but where she currently was as well. Phykira walked in and sat down; waiting patiently until he became aware of her sitting there, just watching him pace like a madman, and with a frown, sat down beside from her. "How Phykira? How did she get away? I sealed the door, I know I did. Didn't I?"

She turned to him. "Yes, you did. I was there, Vincent, and you sealed that door, so I have no idea how she got away. We will find her, and don't worry; we still have the others, so she'll have to come back for them."

He hadn't thought of it that way. It had been his original intent to capture all of them first, but after nearly four years of searching for Aurica, he'd abandoned that plan just for the opportunity to kidnap the annoying girl. With his original plan back in place, he once again set his sights on Ariliria.

~~~~~~~

Aurica awoke in a bright hospital room. A nurse was in the room and was pleased that she had finally awoken. "Don't push it. My name is

Syria, and you're in a hospital, as I'm sure you've realized. A young couple found you unconscious in a nearby park, and was worried when you weren't responding. Do you have any family here? I know this is a private and personal question, but did you run away from an abusive household?"

Aurica was still trying to figure out how she was out of Vincent's clutches. "In a park? I'm not sure how I got there. No, my parents are dead, and my sister is with a jerk. My brother is in their custody for now, but I'll get him back."

The nurse wasn't expecting that kind of situation. "Okay, well you've clearly been through a lot, so I'll have a doctor come in immediately."

The nurse left as fast as she could. Rolling her eyes as the woman stepped out of the room, Aurica pinched her cheek, sighing as she realized that it wasn't a dream. Slipping from the bed, she found her clothes; dressing quickly, before she took one last look around the room and left through the window.

~~~~~~

About the Author

Inspired at a young age by a love of fantasy, science fiction and anime, E.A. Calhoun began her writing career soon after graduating from high school. Balancing her writing between furthering her education and working jobs in sales and early-childhood education, she sought to bring the vast world inside of her head to everyone around her. A graduate of The University of Wisconsin-River Falls, Calhoun has used her degrees in art and education to bring a rich, diverse, alternate universe full of dragons and their human counterparts to life with her Chronicles series.

A lover of art, crafts and the natural world around her, Calhoun can often be found with her head bent over her drawing pad, creating vivid, visual representations of the amazing world inside her head. When she isn't writing, Calhoun enjoys watching movies, spending time with her family and taking long drives through nature while she listens to Ed Sheeran. Calhoun currently resides in Minnesota with her family and a bearded dragon named Ignis. The Chronicles of Azelia is her debut novel.

Calhoun loves hearing from her readers! Connect with her below!
Facebook E.A Calhoun

Printed in the United States
By Bookmasters